One Northern Soul

J R Endeacott

route

J R Endeacott

J R Endeacott was born on April Fools' Day, 1965. He was raised in Beeston, South Leeds and still lives within a (mighty) half-brick's throw of the Elland Road football ground.

First Published in 2002 by Route
School Lane, Glasshoughton, West Yorks, WF10 4QH
e-mail: books@route-online.com

ISBN: 1 901927 17 2

Cover Design: Andy Campbell
Cover Image: © Andrew Varley

Editor: Steve Dearden

Support::
Ian Daley, Lorna Hey, Stuart Sandiforth

Printed by Bookmarque Ltd, Croydon, Surrey

A catalogue for this book is available from the British Library

One Northern Soul was created as part of The Opening Line, a writer
development project run by Yorkshire Art Circus in partnership with the
Word Hoard. The Opening Line was funded by the National Lottery
through the Arts for Everyone scheme.

Full details of the Route programme of books
and live events can be found on our website
www.route-online.com

Route is the fiction imprint of YAC, a registered charity No 1007443

YAC is supported by
Yorkshire Arts, Wakefield MDC, West Yorkshire Grants

*To my family and friends,
and to those who have lost loved ones
at football matches.*

From a pocket I called my heart, I drew a story of Leeds. Pete Wylie had a 'Story of the Blues', this was a Steve Bottomley story of The Whites.

'David Harvey - in for the brilliant but inconsistent Gary Sprake - plucks Neeskens' cross out of the air while Gerd Muller can only look on. Harvey rolls the ball out to Paul Reaney at right back. Reaney quickly squares the ball to Big Jack Charlton who coolly steps over it, allowing it to run to Norman Hunter. His short pass to Terry Cooper at left back eludes the bemused genius Johann Cruyff, who appears to be at odds with the world. Cooper looks down the line, searching for Eddie Gray, but instead plays the ball inside to the nonstop captain Billy Bremner. He swivels and ghosts by Paul Breitner in the centre circle before laying the ball off to his partnering midfield general Johnny Giles. Giles, *visionary* and always aware, sprays it out wide right to 'Hot Shot' Peter Lorimer just inside the opponents' half. He chests it down, gently bounces it on his right thigh and unleashes a thunderbolt volley which flies not towards goal but all the way across the pitch to his fellow Scot, the mercurial Gray on the opposite wing. Gray traps Lorimer's missile dead with his left foot, causing gasps of wonder from the Elland Road faithful and a wry admiring smile from the as yet pedestrian Georgie Best.

Gray, shoulders hunched as always when about to delight fans and dazzle opponents, commences his attack. With feet faster than Fred Astaire, he shimmies and swerves and then breezes by the tormented Ruud Krol. Krol, playing out of his accustomed central position, tries to tackle again to his credit, only to be finished off with a Gray dragback and a deft flick of the ball past him. Gray paces towards the penalty area and curls a pinpoint cross to unsung hero Mick Jones, who gracefully beats Bobby Moore in the air to nod the ball down to Allan 'Sniffer' Clarke. In one fluent movement, the predator Clarke has tapped the ball through the legs of his marker and skipped around him - would you believe it, Franz 'The Kaiser' Beckenbauer 'nutmegged'! Paul Madeley, the Leeds substitute, chuckles with Don

Revie and Les Cocker in the dugout - this was one of Clarke's regular training tricks. The bamboozled Beckenbauer can only watch as Clarke collects the ball near the penalty spot and rifles it past the flailing arms of Dino Zoff, fizzing the net.

Three - nil to Leeds United and it's not even half time yet.'

The story was for my dad, he would've liked to remember Leeds as the footballing kings of Europe. My dad used to tell me how important 'the team behind the team' was at Leeds, meaning the boss Don Revie and his crew, Les Cocker, Syd Owen, Maurice Lindley and even Bob English, who looked like the cheerful granddad of the club to me. And then there were the behind the scenes people too, the overworked and underpaid groundstaff, the laundry women and the admin workers. Once, on a freezing day when the groundsmen were tending to the pitch, Don Revie went out to them to give them each a nip of whisky to warm them up. It was a sign of the family atmosphere the club had at the time and little wonder the pitch was one of the best, suitable for a great side.

My dad took me to Leeds games from the age of four, when I was getting under my mum's feet, and from the (kick) off, I was addicted. It wasn't long before I was pleading to go to all the home games with him. I'd marvel at the four fantastic floodlights, how high they were, and many a time I'd just stand at the foot of one of them, holding on so as not to lose my balance, gazing upwards and getting dizzy at the clouds floating by and the ever so slight sway of the monumental steel structure. When they were switched on at nightime for first team and reserve matches, you could see the glare from miles and miles away and I bet lots of locals saved on their lighting bills. Near to where we entered the stadium was the West Stand façade above the club reception: a rich blue background with the club's coat of arms and LEEDS UNITED A. F. C. in glorious golden lettering over it, just another reminder of the class and sophistication the club had. The cost of my getting in wasn't really a problem for my dad, he had this long grey Mac that he'd smuggle me through the turnstile with, me clamped to his body like a limpet and the wooden rattle stuffed up my jumper digging into my ribs and I'd watch the games seated on his lap.

The team *should* have been the champions of Europe but in football as in life, things don't always turn out as they should. That final against Bayern Munich for instance, should have been just the first European Cup win for Leeds, and ... well there's no need to go on about it just yet. It's safe to say though, that in defeat something died that night - something in the hearts of the players, something in the hearts of the Leeds supporters and people, and possibly football fans around the nation. My dad travelled to the game in Paris and whether it was the injuries he returned with or just his hurt pride, I don't know, but from then on his passion definitely waned and he never went to watch Leeds away from Elland Road again in his life.

There was no recovery from Leeds United after that defeat and in 1979 my dad died from a heart attack, a fucking heart attack. What age was forty-two to have a heart attack? **NO** age, that's what. Me, I was only thirteen at the time; suddenly, without any kind of warning, I'd lost my best friend and my guide for life. Where was the justice? This was the first time anything truly bad had happened to me - the first time I'd encountered death - and no one could tell me *why*. It wasn't fair, it just wasn't fair. God only knows how my mum got through it because I was of little help. I lost count of the number of times I was snapped out of my sleep in the early hours by her sobs from across the landing, every one a pull at my insides. The Bottomley house was not a happy one to be in for a long, long time, I yearned to hear my mum laugh again and I often felt guilty for smiling ever or being remotely cheerful. I couldn't take any of it in properly, it was like I wasn't really here. I begged for none of it to have really happened, that it was all a horrible dream which would disappear when I awoke. Instead of trying to share the grief with my mum and my young brother Andrew, I retreated in to my own personal shadows.

It was the time when my mate Gaz proved how great a friend he was. He was the only person who called for me at our house, who dared mention my dad's death and the only one who had the guts to give me a hug to show how sorry he was about it all. There's no denying it, I was a selfish, thoughtless little shit for some time after, and I spent a lot of the time with Gaz when I should have been home for my mum. He helped me begin enjoying life again and I owed him for it. My dad dying didn't make me go *off the rails* as such, but with the help of Gaz I chose some wrong turnings. At home, I was late to realise I wasn't alone in the darkness.

'You're nicked!' she cried, with more relish than most condiments and spices on sale there.

I half expected to see Reverend Smithie's head pop out St Mary's doors over the road to see what the racket was. Who did she think she was, the fucking Sweeney or what? I just hoped none of the housewives and old dears doing their *legal* shopping knew me as that would've been even worse. **Me** getting caught and with a swag of sweets of all things. Scandalous. Actually, I could have scarpered from the store detective but I'd have had to put her out of the way - and she was old enough to be my gran. I don't know how long it'd taken her to suss me out but it had served me right, I'd been too cocky, thinking the Beeston Co-op was easy pickings. It *was* easy pickings, that's the whole point. I'd always been able to spot store detectives a mile away before, either by the dusty, out of date shopping in their baskets or just by their plain bad acting, but this time like a fart in a trance I'd bloody missed this woman, and in the Co-op of all places, Jesus. Something had gone badly wrong - this shit would never happen to one of my film heroes from the 'pictures' - and it shouldn't have been happening to me.

A hundred yards from the Tommy Wass pub at the foot of 'Miggy' Hill, stood the magnificent Rex Cinema. I loved the Rex; *everyone* loved the Rex. As a sprog, every film I saw there motivated me to race my dad home, who set me off like a whippet - a slow one - with a fifty yards start. Bombing along Old Lane - depending on what we'd just seen, I'd be James Bond, Charlton Heston fleeing the bad Apes or even one of Elvis's characters - instead of my usual Peter Lorimer or Eddie Gray. Even on warm nights my throat throbbed from the coldness of the air I'd gasped and gulped in desperation trying so hard to win. 'This time I'm gonna beat him, this time!' I never did. Whenever 'Battle of Britain' was on, I'd fly home as a Spitfire afterwards, spraying bullets at every human Messerschmitt in my flight path.

Once we saw 'Tom Thumb', showing as part of a special double bill with 'The Wizard of Oz'. My mum had warned me about the 'Yawning Man' character, a little plastocene creation, who made everyone who saw him yawn their heads off. Funnily enough, she was wrong, there was no yawning, only my nodding off. My dad had to carry me all the way home, snoozing in his arms, and after that all the Rex staff treated me like one of the family. There was a friendly silver haired lady in the ticket booth, and a younger dark haired woman in the sweets kiosk with a lovely shining smile. The manager had a little office in the right of the foyer. He was a slim, bald man with black-rimmed glasses and I thought he looked distinguished and important, though he probably had on the same brown suit every time. He used to smile and say, 'Hello, young man', ruffling my hair, (Brian Clough said exactly the same to me once down at Elland Road, but he ruffled my feathers by flying off without giving me his autograph.)

Despite the great times in the Rex, there were lesser quality moments. The Saturday Matinee was nowhere near as good as the Malvern's on Beeston Hill but that was too far away for my little legs to walk. *They* showed the 'Batman' series in full colour, *we* had a Batman that looked crap even to us infants: instead of the brilliant colours and costumes, all we got was a black and *grey* effort with the bat mask looking like it had two upturned ice-cream cornets for ears stuck on it. And our 'serious' films were 'The Famous Five Find a Library Ticket' and 'Flash Gordon Fights Loads of Saps in Metal Skirts from Planet Ridiculous' and shit. At least **every** Saturday Matinee had to put up with Keith Chegwin, it wasn't just us Rex kids. Fucking Keith Chegwin, Pinewood's hope for Hollywood, it was like he was in every Children's Film Foundation flick since 1970 and a shining star he fundamentally wasn't.

'Kes' was the film that had an unexpected effect on me, bigger and longer lasting than any others. The kid in it, Billy, was a loner and a rebel and in one of the first scenes nicked sweets from the shop he delivers for. So it shouldn't take a genius to work out where my shoplifting habits originated. Okay, I was only one example but you still get these so-called intellectuals spouting on that films can't influence people. Everyone's entitled to an opinion but if they're not made to influence people then why do we get millions of commercials rammed in our faces, answer me that, Einstein?

Back in the Co-op, if I'd been anything like Billy in 'Kes' I would've shot off faster than a ferret down a rabbit hole - plus a courteous 'Get stuffed' to the store detective - but I didn't have enough face to do that. In the end, she believed my excuse for stealing, which was just as well as I never could lie for toffee. The thing was, I never got much pocket money and like a knob I usually put my 'earnings' in to the Mill Hill slots rather than into an account and as it was coming up to Christmas, I'd started to pocket my 43p dinner money for presents. I'd cadge crisps and fizzy Mojos off mates for my lunch and then steal whatever took my fancy after school from the Co-op. It went on like that for weeks; I was like the proverbial kid in a sweet shop, except this was a blooming great supermarket. It was a good thing I'd been caught locally and not in town because the police were called in straight away in those places, no messing. My Co-op 'prat catcher' offered me a deal: the choice was, as I'd nicked £1.07 worth of chocolate bars and Opal Fruits I could either go home to fetch what I owed (and inform my mum while I was at it) or stay there while she rang the law. Some choice, I must have run home and back in record time to her little office, sweating like a pig, panting like a dog. I duly paid up and said thank you to her - I did, really - and then I walked home feeling relieved that it was only my appetite I'd just lost. The next time I saw her I planned on saying hello but I never got the chance. From what I gathered, she worked as a for-hire detective in different stores all over Leeds. **I'd** have been good at that job, except I suppose it would be like giving Ronnie Biggs a job as a security guard for British Rail or something.

I'd made some serious money when I was nicking proper gear. Well, serious for a fourteen-plus year old anyway. Football kits, Adidas trainers, Beckenbauer Super football boots (complete with red screw in studs), books, darts, tapes, football stickers by the tray load, you name it, I'd swiped it. Anything anyone wanted, I'd half-inch it in town and sell it to them for a generous price. A thirty-five quid aluminium tennis racquet once, right from the window display under the noses of the Saturday staff at Thornbury's. Brilliant: I got a tenner off of

Tigger for it. Dead proud of that one, I was.

My all time favourite haul though was a box of LPs from HMV. Boxes were piled up all over the shop and with none of the staff bothering about them, I thought they needed some attention so I took off my Harrington, spread it over one box and walked out with it under my arm. They weighed a ton but the adrenalin rush had built me up. Was I chuffed when I tore the box open in my bedroom to find nearly forty albums by The Stranglers called 'La Folie'. I mean, I could have ended up with forty Shakin' shiting Stevens LPs. I kept two of the albums for myself - one still shrink-wrapped in the polythene - and sold the rest for two quid each. It had their biggest hit 'Golden Brown' on so they were easy to get rid of.

Everyone used to think I was brave stealing and in a way, I suppose they weren't far wrong, though I didn't feel that brave. I was always nervous doing it, nearly always needing a crap before a spree. Shoplifting wasn't difficult, you just needed to know what you were doing and keep your nerve - I saw harder lads than me bottle out a few times - it was only *outside* a store and past the checkouts when they could actually arrest you. Everyone always said Woolworths' was the hardest place due to all the 'Dalek' cameras hanging off the ceiling. Yeah right, so there was some poor sap having to watch every customer on every screen every minute of every day, trying to spot shoplifters. I *don't* think.

I never felt guilty for thieving from the big stores, they could afford it and they shouldn't have charged so much for the goods in the first place, except the Co-op I suppose, but I got my comeuppance in the end so justice was done. Woolworths' *asked* for it, on account of the cameras, like when they make it so obvious they want you to do something wrong, you do it. It worked that way for me, anyway. Half of the stores I frequented closed down in the long run, places like Vallances and that one HMV next to Whitelock's alley, and Lillywhite's around the corner, and John Menzies in the same arcade and Scene and Heard Records next to one of Tetley's (least) *finest*, the Precinct. I did feel guilty about pilfering from little shops in Beeston, like Spinks's on Theodore Street and a couple below Cross Flatts Park, only because there were loads of us doing it and it was almost like we had a vendetta against the owners (which wasn't the case, they were usually nice old or middle aged sorts). We never went near Metcalfe's shop or Hurley's off-licence as we knew the families. It all got embarrassing, with four or five of us on a regular basis tactically positioning ourselves in shops, with 'spends' of sixpence between us, handling and scrutinizing bars of chocolate as if we were checking the ingredients and had a view to buying. They never stood a chance, the sweets were nearly too hard to swallow, it was that easy - but not quite - we had no shame, like locusts in rich fields of confectionery. Eventually, and I mean eventually, like after a whole year, the owners caught on and installed glass cases for the goffers to be viewed and not handled. From then on, their profits soared I'm sure, or more likely their losses floored.

I spent most of my profits on Space Invaders, pinball machines and PacMan, in the arcade on Mill Hill, and a gambling game with little metal horses racing around a track, where you put in ten pee to bet on which colour horse you thought would win. After quids and quids I actually did it, I won the prize. Out it popped, a lovely glowing golden box: ten Benson and Hedges cigs. Brilliant, I never even chuffing smoked. I used to spend hours in the amusements, often going in during daylight and resurfacing into the dark. I'd play so many games I became hooked and it didn't matter that I was throwing small fortunes away, so long as I had my regular fix of video game 'ecstacy'. My clothes would be damp with my sweat and I'd struggle to relax for hours afterwards, repeating the various battles and chases I'd been involved with in this dazzling and addictive world of spectacular colours and electronic graphics. The arcade was a good way of spending the cash because my mum would have asked questions at all the coin I was in possession of. If I'd been as clever as I'd considered myself, my life savings would have been much more than the fifty-odd quid or so. When I was really flush, I sometimes put a few pound notes back in to my mum's purse, depending on my mood. I know it's sad but who cares, I felt better for it and it was my way of making up for the too frequent illicit visits I'd made to the kitchen drawer where it was kept along with the tea towels and dishcloths. I always made it clear to my mates that I robbed from shops, not from people, not from *them*, so they could trust me. And because Gaz was my best mate, no one ever tried to bully me in to supplying stuff for free.

The bastards knocked the Rex down to build a new housing estate. No offence to the people who live there but couldn't the bleeding planners have built *around* the cinema? Just seeing the big illuminated REX in bright red on the front of the picture house had always been exciting for me, a bit like fun fair lights at Blackpool or even the less impressive ones at Hunslet feasts. Inside it was always spotless and smelt of polish; everything was in varying shades of red: all the doors were painted in red gloss, the carpet was a plush, deep red, the wallpaper red flock, the big seats and armrests that gave me pins and needles were red, and even the massive velvet screen curtains were, with gold trim and a frilled edge running across the bottom. On the stairs down to the stalls, the floorboards creaked softly, causing you to bounce gently as you walked. They always reminded me of 'The Aristocats' cartoon when cool moggies playing jazz upstairs in a house were stomping so much that the floor gave way. I never went up to the balcony in the Rex so I couldn't tell, but I bet those steps weren't half as much fun as the downstairs ones. After the *curtain fell* on my dad's life, I would have liked to have taken our Andrew to the pictures just like my dad had done with me but the Leeds ABC and ODEONs were too expensive and a bus ride away.

Even though I shoplifted, I'd have really bollocked our kid if he ever tried it, bollocks to whatever the influence on him was to do it. That old saying, 'Do as I say, not as I do' was spot on - I'd done whatever I wanted but I wasn't going to let him be like me. Maybe it was down to what my Uncle Geoff had said to me after the funeral, that now I was the man of the house I should start acting like it. I think I did become more responsible, and I finally started to grow up. I stopped the thieving and I worked harder at school, though by then it was too late.

I knocked school on the afternoon of the match, the coach was due to set off at three and none of the teachers would've noticed my absence, I think they'd given up with me at last. No amount of their preaching the importance of O levels or CSEs could change what we all knew, that there were no jobs worth going for. There didn't seem much point in learning stuff I didn't enjoy and had no chance of improving the odds of my getting decent work. So English, Art and Games were my subjects, the ones I worked hard at, and one of my favourite *out of school* subjects was spitting. Walking down to school on a morning, me and Gaz used to play a game called 'Headers'. It was filthy but it was piss funny an' all, snooking up big rubbery greenies and launching them in to the air, shouting 'Headers' when they were in flight. Watching each other dive out of the way of plummeting spitbombs like demented hunchbacks was ace.

It was never what you could call pleasant, feeling someone's warm phlegm landing in your hair or down your neck. For some reason we thought spitting - or gobbing or whatever you want to call it - made you look tougher. It didn't though, it made you look like a dirty bastard, that's all and it happened all the time at Leeds games, mainly away ones, whenever coppers walked in to our end of the ground. You prayed they'd stay away from you, not because you were scared of getting nicked or clouted but because you didn't want to have to swim in the showers of saliva and phlegm aimed at them. It was unbelievable how much fluid a bloke could produce in such a short space of opportunity - so much spit and snot - and so accurate with their missiles. Poor sods those coppers, I always felt sorry for them. It got even worse a couple of years later during the Miners Strike, thanks to their brethren in the London Met, the real animals. These Cockney coppers who genuinely earned the popular term for the police: Pigs. Maggie Thatcher sent them up to beat down the miners' picket lines and not only were they chuffed at getting paid rakes of overtime, they could get stuck in to the thick Northern bastards for fun as well. AND they got away with it, there was no comeuppance for them boys from the Met, it was just the bobbies in the North who had to suffer the consequences.

I was skint and though I'd given up proper nicking now, I took a few quid out of my mum's purse. She wouldn't've given me it, not for a football match; all she **did** give me was continuous earache about it just being a game. I don't know what she had against it, she never whinged at my dad for watching. Whatever, now she couldn't have stopped me going if she'd tried, it was our biggest match since the European Cup Final against Bayern Munich - when we lost, I cried myself to sleep and my dad came back from Paris the next day with two black eyes and a nasty cut on his nose. I reckoned he'd been smacked with a police baton when the Leeds fans had rioted as the French police didn't like it, specially when millions of ripped out seats were flying at them like lethal frisbees. It should've been the ref getting a beating, not the fans, he was the guilty one, guilty of being crap and guilty of being a crooked bastard.

No matter what, this game versus West Brom was definitely one my dad would've let me go to, even if it meant skipping lessons near exams. In fact, he would've insisted I went: your team needs you through thick and thin, just like your family and friends.

Gaz was supposed to go with me but he bottled it. I was pissed off but he was already on report and one more misdemeanour could get him expelled. We were wasting our time at Matthew Murray High School, but getting expelled would have helped no one. I picked my ticket up from National's station on Wellington Street and might have stayed in their waiting room had it not been so damp and dirty and smelling of piss. Instead, I went for a walk around town and *bought* a Puzzler from WH Smiths, I had definitely reformed.

I've always loved Leeds city centre, it was another world from the suburbs like my Beeston: pen pushers in posh suits and sexy secretaries in short skirts rushing around all over the place. It was forever busy and alive - I'd go mental living in the country, I swear. Walking back on Boar Lane I decided to pop down Mill Hill in to the arcade for a few games of Space Invaders and PacMan to pass a bit more time away.

I returned to the coach station after inflicting sufficient video carnage for one afternoon. Loads more blokes in Leeds scarves were already waiting around, drinking cans of beer. There was a handful of biddies with suitcases as well, looking dead nervous. Somehow, I think they were more likely going to Bournemouth for their jols rather than West Bromwich for beer, football and fighting. You never know though, there were tales of Chelsea's old soldier supporters - the Pensioners - who went to games in their uniforms and medals, wading in with walking sticks a blazing whenever there was any trouble. Do me a favour, it'd be like punching your granddad if you got in a scrap with them.

All the yellow, white and blue scarves and a big Union Jack with LEEDS UNITED in gold sewn on gave me a brilliant buzz of pride - we were all in this battle together.

The same couldn't be said of the coach driver though, he wasn't exactly what you could call team spirited. Four or five lads with beer were pissed off with him - he wouldn't let them bring booze on to the coach. They wouldn't mess with him though, he was a big bloke and his five o'clock shadow and dark looks made him like a character from the Godfather. Everyone could hear them slagging him off from the back seat but he took no notice and by the time we got to West Brom, they'd shouted for a toilet stop a million times. He'd refused, unscheduled stops being a sackable offence, or so he'd said. I reckon he was taking the piss but you had to laugh. I had a window seat, next to a chubby bloke with a tash and greasy black hair. He was on his tod an' all so I had to speak to him a bit though I did my best to concentrate on my Puzzler in peace. It turned out he was one of the most loyal Leeds fans ever, having followed Leeds in nearly a thousand Leeds games home and away on the trot.

It was about five when the driver parked up near the stadium. The drinkers shot off like greyhounds out of their traps, round the back of the coach and pissing like dogs in broad daylight, swearing and groaning, streams of piss and puddles everywhere. There was over two hours before kick off and I didn't have enough money for the pub so I went looking for the away fans' section on my own. I hoped not to attract any attention from West Brom fans as my yellow Leeds shirt and bright blue Harrington jacket made me a sitting duck.

Fortunately, I didn't see any dodgy characters for me to worry about. I walked to the main gates, passing a few fans and hot dog and burger stands on the way. The steam of fried onions and cooked meat wafted over the pavement and smelt delicious, as it always does; not that it ever tastes that good. I wasn't hungry anyway, I was too nervous about the match to eat. I could smell horse muck too, though I never saw any horses. Gaz always liked the smell would you believe but he ate his bogies as well so it shouldn't come as that much of a surprise. I had just enough cash for a match programme and bought one from an old beachball of a bloke in a long sheepskin and flat cap. He must have been sweating cobs because it was a warm evening, specially as he had a black waffle knit jumper on which made his beer gut look even more immense. He was a nice bloke though and I thought his Brummie accent was brilliant. He said he'd loved Leeds when Revie was boss and he should never have left to take the England job. I couldn't fault him, my dad would have agreed and so did I.

As I left he called, 'Yow take care, mite'.

They charged me full price to get in even though I was still at school - it was scandalous (three quid fifty worth of scandal). Most clubs put their prices up for Leeds games because we had more supporters. There was no choice but to accept it but bollocks like this is never justified. I squeezed in through the squealing turnstile, to steps that led up to the terrace entrance. From there I could see a row of houses and neat gardens just a stone's throw away, or should that be brick? I didn't envy the people living in them, not because the houses were old and terraced - thousands the same in Leeds - but because it must've been awful living so close to a footie ground, with all the away fans nosing in your front room every week. Worse if they were Scousers, they'd nick anything they could get their hands on **and** piss on your doorstep to demonstrate that famous sense of humour.

There were about two hundred Leeds fans packed together in the stadium, if that's what you'd call ancient concrete and bricks and corrugated roof. We were situated in a corner, fenced in and segregated from the home fans. There was a peaceful buzz of people talking, no chants or songs yet, sort of like they were waiting for more guests to arrive at a party. At home in the Kop it regularly got so crammed you could easy be carried off your feet in tumbles which could be a laugh, unless you got sucked in and dragged to the floor or you splattered into a barrier. This night I decided to stand at the back, safer that way I decided. While the light was good enough I leant back on the cold metal of a barrier and flicked through the programme, looking at the mostly cheap black and white photos and soaking in the warm breezes of Bovril and crusty meat pies. The DJ's disco records, the floodlights flickering to life, players warming up and the ball boys fagging the balls stirred the crowd, and soon pockets of Leeds and West Brom fans were goading each other through the fencing. By now our corner was pretty much full with mostly fellas, though there was a smattering of women. There was no one younger than me that I could see and that made me more nervous. I heard a vocal rumble which grew in to a roar of the 'Leeds Leeds Leeds' chant. It was like we'd woken up at last, and Leeds songs started to rise from everywhere.

Here we go with Leeds United
We're gonna give the boys a hand
Stand up and sing for Leeds United
We are the greatest in the land

Every day, we're all gonna say
We love you Leeds! Leeds! Leeds!
Everywhere, we're gonna be there
We love you Leeds! Leeds! Leeds!

Marchin' on together
We're gonna see you win (na, na, na, na, na, na)
We are so proud
We shout it out loud
We love you Leeds! Leeds! Leeds!

We've been through it all together
And we've had our ups and downs (ups and downs!)

We're gonna stay with you forever
At least until the world stops going round

Every day, we're all gonna say
We love you Leeds! Leeds! Leeds!
Everywhere, we're gonna be there
We love you Leeds! Leeds! Leeds!
Marchin' on together
We're gonna see you win (na, na, na, na, na, na)
We are so proud
We shout it out loud
We love you LEEDS! LEEDS! LEEDS!

I've always loved the songs. 'Yorkshire Republican Army', it gave me goose pimples whenever we sang it. Not in the same way as the Beatles songs, this was real adrenalin pride, chanting the one verse over and over…

Y - R - A!
We're Yorkshire's Republican Army,
We're barmy,
Wherever we go, we fear no foe,
For we are the
Y - R - A!

Tonight's main song would be about West Brom, to the tune of 'I Do Like to be Beside the Seaside'.

Oh I do like to be beside the seaside
Oh I do like to be beside the sea
Oh I do like to walk along the prom prom prom
Where the brass band plays 'Fuck off West Brom'

FUCK OFF WEST BROM,
FUCK OFF WEST BROM,
FUCK OFF WEST BROM…

And it goes on like that until we get bored or arrested. Love it.

I felt confident, I couldn't see us losing if the players had enough passion - Allan Clarke would make sure they did. We'd never been thrashed all season but we'd lost a lot of games by the odd goal or drew when we should've won. Even the Saturday before, we beat Brighton and we thought we were safe, but the other bottom teams won so we were no better off. Tonight was the moment of truth, I hoped the players didn't bottle it. As I looked at my watch urging the time to speed up, loads of police streamed in around the pitch from the opposite corner towards us. I looked around me and there were about thirty black uniforms behind us. The ref blew his whistle to start the game. We waited, for Leeds to do something, to show that the players did care and that the glory years of Revie's team weren't just distant memories. Leeds dropping into Division Two would be like a royal death, only worse.

We went close to scoring a couple of times in the first twenty minutes. Gary Hamson had a thirty yarder well saved and Kenny Burns just failed to reach a cross in front of goal - he would've got to it if he hadn't've been so bleeding fat - but it was easy to see why both teams were so low in the league. We only needed a draw but the players hardly seem bothered, I couldn't believe it. Before, when Billy Bremner pulled on the number four shirt you knew he'd give his all for Leeds, for Don Revie, for the supporters and for the whole bloody city. He'd never give up 'til the final whistle: ***Keep on Fighting***. There was hardly any of that tonight, no spirit or guts and the players were nearly always second best. We chanted and sang to spur them on, *'Come on Leeds! Come on Leeds!'* but it didn't work. The longer the match went on the more aggravated we got, with more pushing and shoving and threats between the rival fans.

Suddenly, there was this loud clang above us like a big block of cement landing on metal. The swaying and jostling got worse and a spill of people made me lose my balance and bump the bloke in front of me, a big skinhead in an olive green jacket and swastika on the arm. And as nazi fuckwits do, he picked on the nearest and smallest person to him. He stared at me as if I've done it on purpose and I was shitting my pants. I said sorry but he carried on giving me daggers and I carried on bricking it - even after he turned back I didn't feel safe - *fucking hell we're supposed to be on the same side*. And then West Brom scored and most of the ground exploded with a roar, a horrible feeling, as if thousands of people were taking the piss. The police seemed to enjoy it as well as they prodded and pushed us in the back with their truncheons. I looked puzzled at one of them to find out what his game was but he just called me a Leeds bastard, telling me to watch the match. And then he poked me in the back harder, and I fell forward, in to the twatting skinhead again. I froze as he turned around and grunted 'Stop fucking pushing' and he punched me **hard** - like a warm half brick slammed into my nose. I fell back, banging my head on someone's shins as I landed on my backside. The legs were that copper's and he yanked me up. I was nearly grateful and like a tit thought he was going to help me but before I knew it he was dragging me away and down some steps, pushing me out of the ground through a big iron gate. I pleaded with him but he just told me to piss off home, slamming the gate in my face. The pain really kicked in: my head pounding and my nose throbbing like a bastard. I gagged with the thickness of blood and snot flooding my head and I shook like a shiting dog. I spat in disgust on to a turnstile door but that just made me feel more pathetic. Now I knew where my urge to spit on people in authority or who piss me off came from. Outside the stadium it was eerie, there was no one else around and the sound of the crowd felt miles away. I was wishing I was at home with my mum and our kid - even with the nagging and shit - and I burst out crying. I couldn't help it, my voice whining an' all, it was sickening hearing myself doing it. The first time since my dad died and it was not to be the last. I trudged off to find the coach, launching missiles of blood and snot in to the floodlit air. The driver was a Leeds fan after all; he was listening to the match on the radio when he opened the coach door for me. He was also a decent bloke - about the same age as my dad would have been - cleaning my bloodied face with cotton wool and head-clearing, stinging antisceptic. While he was tending to me, the radio commentatator screamed that West Brom had scored again. It didn't matter as much as I'd've expected - I couldn't feel any more bastarding pain if I'd tried. Fucking 1982 what a great year; I leave school for what and Leeds get relegated.

The journey back was dark and lonely and dragged forever. Hardly anyone said a word on the coach, not even the bloke next to me. I felt bad for him because it meant even more to him than to me and I never thought that possible. Later on we heard there'd been about eighty or so Leeds fans arrested, for fighting and ripping down the fences and invading the pitch. A couple of coppers got done in an' all and sad to say it, I really hoped one of them was the bastard who'd shafted me. We got back at about one in the morning and the driver went out of his way to drop me near our house. It might not seem like much but I was dead grateful to him, they usually drop you in town, miles away. From the bottom of our street I could see our yellow living room curtains glowing in the orange darkness, meaning my mum was still up. In a way it was a relief - I'd forgotten my key and I knew I was in for a bollocking - I didn't want to get her out of bed to receive it. The door was unlocked. I crept in and found her awake in the armchair in her horrible blue wool dressing gown and even more horrible pink rollers. She was a good looking woman my mum, but not in that get up, and her mood was no prettier. Before she could finish demanding to know where the hell had I been I was kneeling next to her, head on her lap with it all flooding out, crying and apologising. She stroked my head and said I'd get over it, and then twice she said it, her favourite, 'It's only a game'. And you know what? I laughed, I did, I actually laughed.

We'd had it planned for weeks and all our mates in the Matthew Murray Fifth Form knew. We were looking forward to it, just like Christmas really, and the prospect had helped ease some of the pain of Leeds United getting relegated. But come the big day only five of us turned up. I was disgusted, be it only briefly as we had just 45 minutes to drink, be merry and return to school to wreak havoc, or whatever, and there was no point me whinging, or time to do it. Dul from Holbeck, Docko from Miggy, Gaz from Belle Isle and Bruges and me from Beeston managed to make it. These lads were now even higher in my estimations and it had nothing to do with their nicknames. With a surname like Bottomley, I should be grateful I didn't have one, though I was jealous of those who did as it made them sound cooler and more popular. Docko's was obvious: Paul Dockerty. Dul's not so: Dean Abbott was his real name and due to his wearing a long and smelly Afghan coat we called him Abdul and then just 'Dul' for short. He was the youngest hippy I ever met and he appeared to be trying to grow his hair like Brian May's. I liked the name Bruges best: Craig Robinson used to wear a punky black and white hooped mohair like The Damned wore and he had a typical teenager effort of a moustache which just looked like his top lip needed a good scrubbing. Someone declared that the jumper and the tash made him look French and so they called him 'Bruges'. Everyone knew where Bruges was really but 'Paris' or 'Marseille' didn't have the same ... *je ne sais quoi* to it.

We ran from school when the tannoyed dinner chimes rang, through the terraced streets of ye olde Holbeck and surprised a milkman on the way by not shouting abuse at him. We walked casually into a man's domain called The Spotted Cow on Domestic Street. The barman was in his early twenties and totally un-bothered about our age irregularities, made obvious by our collective acne, pathetic facial hair and collection of school books. He served us five pints of lager. Gaz had ordered because he looked the oldest and the rest of us were shy. If he'd wanted, the barman could have easily pissed on our Last Day at School Bonfire, so he was alright by us. He might have been grateful for the business, the Cow was dead.

Nearly everyone I know would like to be a kid again, without the having to go to school bit, most probably. It was obvious that we five hated school. Obvious maybe, but wrong - we loved it - for completely the wrong reasons, of course. We weren't troublemakers, but you could stuff your lessons and rules and half the teachers. As far as we were concerned we were there to have a laugh, simple as that. Matthew Murray High School saw us fail exams with a 'D' for dismally but blimey, we learned to enjoy ourselves. I don't remember many schooldays when I wasn't close to pissing my pants laughing at something someone had said or done. Not that I was a giggling simpleton or anything - I laughed at 'Terry & June' and 'George & Mildred' as much as I did when Bambi's mum bought it in the cartoon - but school life was often stomach achingly funny. For one thing, Docko had an arse you could set your cheapo digital watch by: five minutes in to every morning assembly with the head teachers looking down at you from the stage, he'd let rip with a magnificent rasping fart. It was even more impressive in exams, with everyone quiet and concentrating, up he'd pop with a tremendous trouser ripper. My own arse had always been of great disappointment to me, never being able to produce such impressive bottom sounds. Good old toilet humour, it always brightens the English day. Even Charlie Chaplin had a fart joke in 'The Great Dictator' but no bugger believes me.

Those dinnertime drinks were a celebration, it was the last day at school, *the last day!* The other kids should have thought the same: ***the last day EVER.*** For God's sake, what was wrong with them? The closing page of the final chapter of nigh on twelve years of your life, it had to be commemorated, it was sick not to. I couldn't believe the other kids were actually scared, what did they think the school or the teachers could do to you on your last day there? In the pub we gabbed away like...well, like schoolchildren, and I'll never forget that dinnertime, even though I was pissed by the end of the mammoth three quarters of an hour session. It was the first time I'd realised one of the meanings of life - one of the meanings of life for a Leeds lad, anyway - and that's the importance of the pub. Most of us go to the pub to talk about anything and everything, away from the nagging boss/wife/bird/family, you name it: **'Exist to be pissed'** to quote the equally well named group Serious Drinking. Despite the fact that it's always men who start trouble, be they politicians, pissheads, football supporters or all of the above, you can also rely on them to make friends virtually anywhere in the world, by use of the universal language in a pub or bar. The five main subjects of the universal language of *pub-speak* are: politics, beer, football, women and music, in no particular order. You can throw in secondary topics like films, cartoons, other sports and even the weather, but these five are the most common conversation starters.

Over the four pints of lager we each had, which really was three and a half at the most except for Gaz, we made predictions about futures. None of us knew what we wanted to do work-wise and judging by the (lack of) job opportunities advertised in the Evening Post, it didn't really matter anyway. Fortunately, we each had a bicycle we could hop on so things would turn out nice and rosy for us - on Norman Tebbit's planet anyway, with what he was to say about getting on your bike to find work. Keep on pedalling Mr Tebbitt, right until you get to the white cliffs of Dover, and then pedal that little bit faster, you fucking tosser. Fair do's, it's easy blaming the government and teachers for our lack of personal ambition but in truth none of us had a clue what we wanted to do. We'd always wanted to be footballers and actors and athletes but that would only ever happen on Planet Norman, not in our real red brick world of South Leeds. Docko's *immediate* ambition was to punch some of the lads he hated, the ones who'd forever picked on him, and then turn his attentions to the older bullies, the *teachers* who'd picked on him more while getting paid for it. He forgot, bless him, that he was less capable of looking after himself in a fight than a new born foal or Bambi on ice. Gaz was planning to have a kip at his desk in maths and Bruges was debating whether to go straight home or not. Dul wanted to stay in the pub seeing as he lived only a few doors down from it. Not surprisingly, I admired his intentions the most, and virtually had to drag him back to school after, chuckling and protesting. We held votes on who would win certain categories like an Oscars ceremony:

'**Most Likely to be a Pisshead**' was no contest, we each came equal first in that one.

'**Most Likely to be a Puff**' went to Trevor Moscroft who, if he didn't turn out that way, certainly did a good impersonation of a young Quentin Crisp. He also won the '**Boy Most Likely to Dress in Women's Clothing**' category.

'**Most Likely to be Famous**' was changed to 'Infamous', as in a Ripper or Myra Hindley way, and was awarded to 'Fuck Off' Brooksy, who seemed to have no friends, nor did he want any, and his warmest greeting to people was 'Fuck off', even the teachers.

We were gonna have a '**Most Likely to be Young Single Mum**' title, until Bruges pointed out why we'd not seen Sarah Browne at school for most of the year.

Last - and least - was '**Most Likely to be a Tory**'. We struggled with that one but eventually decided to award it to Moscroft again. Cruel? So right but then again, a cross-dressing Tory queer? Surely, things like that didn't happen in those circles?

It began to hit home that while my mouth was celebrating, inside I felt I was at a funeral just about - I was going to miss so many people, some in fact I would never see again in my life, like Dul for instance. I'd even miss some of the teachers and some of the girls who I *didn't* fancy, like Caz and Joan, and Narinda and Jill. And Miss Scheider my form teacher, I'd miss seeing her (mostly her small but perfect figure, I must admit). And those lasses I *did* fancy, God I was going to miss them alright. If there'd been an exam in it, I'd have gained an A-plus in self-abuse, that was a dead cert. How I regretted not having the nerve to ask them to go out with me or not telling them how much I'd craved their attentions.

We staggered back to school, half drunkenly, half exaggerating the effect of the drink, ten minutes late, which was quite considerate of us we thought, considering the circumstances. We weren't the last but we definitely were the most pissed. Our Headmaster, Mr Kerr, was waiting at the gates for us, like a worried father watching out for his brood. Shit, I bet he was impressed with me, especially when I greeted him warmly and courteously with a bow, and his identical transparent twin standing at his side. Besides Gaz, who did fall asleep, I don't know what the others got up to that afternoon. Nothing, I bet. I sat at the back of maths with Mr Akeroyd, befuddled even more than normal, blinking and trying to focus properly. Word soon spread around the classroom that I was drunk, and all the kids kept looking around at me to see if I'd do anything out of the ordinary (like get a question right, maybe). Even Lem next to me was impressed which made a change from most of that year where I think I'd de-pressed him with my time wasting. I just smiled at them all, I wasn't going to talk in case I sounded like a berk. After the lesson I tried to apologise to Mr Akeroyd for my behaviour. He wasn't fussed, I don't think he gave a toss about me really, not by then anyway. Looking back, I can't say I blame him, I never gave a toss myself either, well not sober. I swayed out of his classroom and slid my way along the glossed corridor walls of the school, unable to walk straight or upright. I met the lovely Linda Braithwaite on the way, looking even lovelier than normal. I told her how beautiful she was and how I'd always dreamed about her, and I declared my true and undying love for her. She couldn't understand one word I said.

Mr Kerr had got me in his office some time before, as I was an 'underachiever' whose performance was cause for concern to the teachers. They weren't concerned at all, they were just trying to get me into trouble, I knew their game. I didn't get a bollocking, Mr Kerr was very civil and okay about it, putting me off my guard from the start by inviting me to sit down, in a comfy chair. His reputation was as a hard as nails Scot, and you don't cross them, they had a habit of headbutting or glassing people. He did come across as hard but fair with it and I liked that. I think he was strangely impressed with me, too - the only thing I wasn't underachieving in was underachieving. *I* wasn't impressed though: the two subjects I liked and worked at properly were English and Art, and I'd been reported in them an' all which wasn't fair. Umbrage was all I took from the meeting I'm sorry to report - instead of letting him help me, I took bloody umbrage - I wasn't underachieving in immaturity either, that became obvious. What he should have done was talk to me bluntly, *threatened* me even, like *'Listen, you wee tosspot, pull your finger out and stop trying to fuck up*

*your life. If you don't sort yourself out, I'll make haggis of your sorry little
arse. Ye ken?'*

I'd have listened then and it would have done more than the
Careers Interview we had, what a joke that was. It wasn't the fella's
fault but when you don't know what you want to do and you think
there's more prospect in digging for gold in Cross Flatts Park than
there is of unearthing a career, his question 'What do you want to
Do?' deserved nothing more than 'I'm off to be a doley'. I didn't of
course, I thought better of it, proving it with a shrug of my
shoulders and 'I don't know.'

Mr Kerr died not long after I'd left Matthew Murray High and he
was the head of another high school. I read about it in the Evening
Post when I was looking for a job. I was sorry: for one thing, he
wasn't that old. I respected him and hoped he died happy.

My mum was close but no Castella to the truth about football: it **was** more than just a game, a lot more. Having said that, relegation of your club, heartbreaking as it genuinely is, is nothing compared to the death of a loved one; Leeds United had suffered from a serious illness but they'd stay alive with me forever.

I don't know the first time Leeds fans had sung it. My earliest memory of hearing it was away at Grimsby Town, our first game back after a not long enough absence in the Second Division. The chant went on for ages and ages, and the noise we made - helped by the echoing of the covered terrace we stood on - created a massive atmosphere. If it had been sung before, which I doubt, no way could it have been as loud or as passionate as today.

We are the Champions - Champions of Europe
We are the Champions - Champions of Europe

In the early seventies, English football was just about the best around and even Celtic/Rangers land wasn't bad either. European clubs like Ajax and Bayern Munich and Barcelona and Juventus *etcetera*, would disagree but the English League was making its mark on Europe - and I don't mean the supporters, they'd take their chance later. From the late sixties, Leeds had made regular sorties in to Europe, battling for the Inter City Fairs Cup (later the UEFA Cup), the Cup Winners Cup and the ultimate prize, the European Cup.

We are the Champions - Champions of Europe
We are the Champions - Champions of Europe
We are the Champions - Champions of Europe

Billy and the boys did us proud, they did the country proud, and the loyal travelling hordes did too, on their journeys to new lands, new worlds even, without hardly a whiff of trouble or violent intent.

Not only was the quality of English football great and proud in those days, I always had the feeling that overall, even though run by old farts more likely to kick the bucket, the game itself was clean - there was no bribing officials, no match fixing, no *cheating*.

We are the Champions - Champions of Europe
We are the Champions - Champions of Europe

NOW JUST THE LEFT   *We are the Champions*

THEN THE RIGHT   *Champions of Europe,*

AND SO ONWARDS   *We are the Champions*

Champions of Europe

Course, if you're lucky enough, memories from your childhood are pleasant, possibly rosier than reality, but you can't tell me English football was dishonest or tainted too badly, not with players like Keegan and Hunter and the Charlton brothers and Eddie Gray and Bell and Ball and Mackay and Jennings and Law and scores of others, all prominent and highly respected footballers who played football with determination and loyalty. And not forgetting Bobby Moore, despite his apparent liking for shoplifting in Colombia.

We are the Champions
Champions of Europe,
We are the Champions
Champions of Europe,
We are the Champions
Champions of Europe

Unfortunately, the same cleanliness isn't something commonly associated with many foreign opponents or referees. Don't get me wrong, English referees could be a bad joke - whether their guide dog wagged its tail or not - but you could never label them as crooked or bent. Mistakes happened - as their parents often owned up to, no doubt - but taking bribes? Nah, not here. Wake up, this was England.

We are the Champions
Champions of Europe,
We are the Champions
Champions of Europe,
We are the Champions
Champions of Europe,
We are the Champions
Champions of Europe,
We are the Champions
Champions of Europe,
We are the Champions
Champions of Europe

Leeds were conned in Europe a few times. I bet other clubs such as Liverpool, Forest, Arsenal and co suffered the same way an' all. Whether it was bribing match officials, players diving like they've been snipered, off the ball 'incidents' or a country's authorities tampering with the food or letting their supporters hold street parties at fucking four in the morning near the English's hotel, it happened regularly.

We are the Champions
Champions of Europe,
We are the Champions
Champions of Europe,
NOW GRADUALLY FASTER, LOUDER
We are the Champions
Champions of Europe,
We are the Champions
Champions of Europe,
We are the Champions
Champions of Europe

There was a lot of hurt pride and passion in the air on the Leeds terracing at the time of the Grimsby game, having been relegated months before, so who in their right minds would set a fixture for the *new* Leeds United and their droves of followers on the opening day of a new season in August on a Saturday near the seaside? Now let's have a think about it. Oh yes, that's right, the Football League, that's who. I mean, summer and the seaside and beer and Friday nights had never been traditional hot spots *on their own*, had they? The Second Division was full of places and pubs and football grounds the fans had never been to before - the gloom of failure on the pitch was soon outshone by the anticipation of new territories to explore and new adventures aplenty in store. I'd like to shake the hands of the fellas who made the chant what it was to become. Previously unheard power and velocity, combined with punches in the air in time with your line - I swear, the ground shook. If you were in the crowd with us, you **were** Leeds and you were One of the Champions, and a Champion of Europe.

We are the Champions	This is for Referee Tinkler
Champions of Europe,	**On the side of West Brom**
We are the Champions	
Champions of Europe,	

We are the Champions	This is to England for taking Don Revie
Champions of Europe,	And treating him like a dog
We are the Champions	
Champions of Europe,	This is for us selling Tony Currie
We are the Champions	What a waste
Champions of Europe,	
We are the Champions	And Duncan McKenzie
Champions of Europe,	Nearly as bad
We are the Champions	
Champions of Europe,	This is for 44 days of Clough
We are the Champions	It should have been none
Champions of Europe,	

We are the Champions
Champions of Europe!
We are the Champions
Champions of Europe!
We are the Champions
Champions of Europe!

This is for the ban in Europe
and for Greece 73, bent referee

This is for 75,
stick your offside

WE ARE THE CHAMPIONS
CHAMPIONS OF EUROPE!
WE ARE THE CHAMPIONS
CHAMPIONS OF EUROPE!
WE ARE THE CHAMPIONS
CHAMPIONS OF EUROPE!
WE ARE THE CHAMPIONS,
CHAMPIONS OF EUROPE!
WE ARE THE CHAMPIONS
CHAMPIONS OF EUROPE!

Thank you ma'am, did the earth move for you?

I shouldn't have hit him, I know that, but who's never made a big mistake in their life? The shithead had wound me up and it wasn't the first time, he'd done it before at Matthew Murray for God knows how many months. If anyone wants to know, I tell them that I kicked the crap out of a racist in a curry house and it's the truth, well mostly. I mean, Cockram *was* a racist, he'd made that plain by plastering NF stickers all over the school, and I did batter him, though he got his own back in the end. Thing is, I was racist too, not like the fascist and nazi scum handing out their filth in town and at the football, but deep down, I was. When you see a black fella walking towards you, what's the first thing you see, the very first; what enters your mind? It's that he's black, that's what, and then the rest of his features register. It's true. No, not exactly racist but it is noticing someone's skin colour before any other aspect so it is a genuine *natural* racism.

Me calling the football team from below Cross Flatts Park 'the Pakis' was racist, to some people. For me it really was just a word short for 'Pakistani', nothing more. I know people say that you can't say *'It's just a word'* because it has more meaning than that, but it **was** just a word when **I** said it, and no one but me knew what went on in my head when I did use it. I appreciated their point of view, though and the last thing I wanted was to be compared with those wankers with their leaflets and stupid salutes so I stopped saying 'Paki' and used 'Asian' instead. It was like calling a Jock, sorry Scot, a Briton - they'd be dead chuffed with that, I'm sure - or us English classed as Europeans: yeah, right on, we're all the same aren't we, none of us looks different.

I never knew where half of the Asian lads were from: Pakistan, India, Bangladesh or England. And that included mates I'd known for years like Ashi and Jaz and Kishor, who I'd known since nursery school. So ignorant yes, that were me but racist - no way, José - never was, never will be. I try and take people for who they are, not what, and I can't see how or why someone can hate a person because of their colour or where they're from, I really can't. Anyone who does think like that is fucked in the head.

So, *why* did I start on him? Well to be honest, there isn't one particular reason. I mean, there was the beer for instance; drunk, I'm normally all smiley and friendly but on this night something snapped and I got nasty. And there *was* the racism, but I couldn't really claim to be a crusader against prejudice and stuff, soapboxes have never been my scene. It could have been because I was jobless, birdless, skint and following a terminally ill football team, or even due to the piss English summer we were having as per normal. There was another possible reason, one I'd not thought of before, and that was because I *could* fight him, and win. Doing him in made me feel like a world-beater and for those very few moments I **loved** the sensation. *'I'm on top of the world, Ma!'*

In the Boston Curry House, there were about a dozen decrepit video games lining the walls and a few plaggy seats to park your bum whilst waiting for your takeaway. A hatch in the wall with a counter underneath was where you placed your orders. The room next door was the restaurant bit, though I'm not sure Egon Ronay would ever want to visit. Me and Gaz had been drinking in town and had caught the last bus home, as we often did when we hadn't pulled (as we often hadn't). We decided on a 'Ruby Murray' and the Boston made easily the best onion bhajis in the history of the Southern (Leeds) Hemisphere. Cockram had used the same bus home as ourselves but I wasn't going to let the wankstain spoil my night if I could help it. I'm not sure whether he purposely went out of his way to follow but in he walked to the Boston, jumped up on to the counter and sat grinning at us as if he'd put one over on us or something. I suppose for those few seconds, he'd succeeded. Those few seconds stretched my patience too far: I told him to move but he just shook his head and smirked at me. Whatever was going on in his head, I don't know, but he was definitely asking for it in mine. I obliged, grabbing him by the collar - he wrenched my arm away way too easily for my liking - he was stronger than I'd expected but before I dwelled on whether I was scared or embarrassed or what I lashed out and punched him on the temple. There was a slight pain in my knuckles as I did it...but I liked the feeling. He dropped on to his right side only to bounce back up like a bleeding Weeble. I noticed the grin had gone at least. I punched him again; he stayed down this time. Gripping his poncey blond fringe I hit him again and again in the face until Gaz dragged me off. He had a hold of me from behind; I was struggling to break free.

'Leave it Steve, he's had enough,' Gaz said.

I was shaking, *buzzing*.

The owner Mani came out from the back, flustered and fussing, 'No fighting, no fighting'.

I looked at Cockram and I admit I was disappointed. I wanted to see blood but there was just a trickle from his mouth and only pink blotches of skin around his eyes and on his forehead. **Why** was Mani looking after him, *Cockram* was the low life in this situation? Cockram sat up straight. Suddenly, in one quick motion he sprang from the counter and head-butted me in the mouth. I reacted by cracking him again; he went sprawling over the grimy vinyl floor, slamming against a Space Invaders. He staggered to his feet and scarpered before I followed it up with a kicking, whelping like a leathered mongrel and threatening to fetch the police. I could taste blood and my front teeth and gums were sore as fuck.

We sat in the restaurant and Gaz ate his curry and most of mine, including the bhajis as my mouth hurt too much. And then two police constables walked in, carrying their helmets under their arms.

Me being an average sort of lad I never thought I'd think that way about someone but looking at the others in the corridor outside court, I did feel I was better than them; they were dregs and I wasn't. I couldn't help it, it was the way they dressed and the way they acted. Not that I was suited up to the nines or anything but at least I had a shirt and tie on and decent kegs. They looked liked they'd dressed as scruffy as possible, in jeans and trainers and that. And course most of them had to have tattoos didn't they? I had nothing against well-designed ones, you know the *artistic* sort, but anyone with CUT HERE next to a row of dots on their neck is a bit of a prick in my book. Obviously, I kept this to myself because they looked like psychos, even the women. A couple of hard faced birds there were definitely prozzies I decided, with their long bleached hair and short skirts. You could see the carpet didn't match the curtains, if you get my drift. I shouldn't say it but I'd have paid them not to have sex if anything.

It wasn't just how people were dressed though, it was the 'Rebel Without a Cause' attitude: smoking when it was No Smoking, staring out coppers and court officials, cracking chewing gum bubbles and shouting and swearing all the time.

What sort of saddo spends their time in court in the Public Gallery for Christ's sake? Cheaper than a bull 'fight' I suppose but just as sick, if not worse. People who do it should take a good long look at themselves and consider why they're here. I shouldn't let trivial stuff like that bother me as fortunately, no one turned up to watch 'The Bottomley Case'. This was good news because it meant it wouldn't be reported in the papers. **That** I don't think I would have handled very well. The Court Attendant had called my name out and led me in to the courtroom. I was standing in the dock with my legs shaking, gripping the bar in front of me to steady myself. I looked up at the three people looking down at me a few yards away: a middle-aged woman seated between two grey haired blokes. They were the Magistrates and she was in charge, I guessed. It hit me just then, before anyone said a word, that *never*, **never**, did I want to be there again. I didn't want to go near thinking about what it must be like facing a long prison sentence, Jesus. There was some touching cloth going on in my undies, I kid not.

But then the lady smiled at me and I felt more relaxed straight away. I thought, 'I'm in here, I'm gonna be alright'. But then she asked me quite an important question: where was my solicitor, Thomas Sugar?

I felt like asking her the same question - shouldn't *they* know? 'I don't know, sorry', I said and she smiled again. For a second, I really thought she might let me off seeing the predicament I was in. I smiled back, hoping.

'Well then Mister Bottomley, would you like to defend yourself?'

What would you have done? Forget that, what would you have done as a clueless, totally bricking it, totally on your lonesome sixteen year old?

'I don't know, sorry,' I said again. She gave me a choice: to carry on and defend myself or arrange another date with my defence in attendance. It wasn't really a choice, I'd have been stupid to defend myself and would probably have ranted on about how the racist/fascist/*whatever-ist* wanker had deserved what he'd got and the book would definitely have been flying through the air in my direction.

My mum rang up the solicitors, I was too flummoxed by it all. Sugar - sorry **Mister** Sugar - was very apologetic for not turning up, blaming some underling in his office for the oversight. I should have punched him when we met again, things would have been more interesting. It was too cold for a suit on the day of my 'retrial', not that I had one anyway, so I wore a navy blue waterproof reversible jacket that looked better than it sounds. He was already waiting for me, fair play to him, in a big room with marble floor and Play School arch windows. It wasn't much warmer than outside, God what must it be like in the nick? He shook my hand but he didn't look happy: he warned me that it was this particular Magistrate's last case of the afternoon and that as yet he hadn't bollocked anybody or even found anyone guilty *all day*. The good news was that it was highly unlikely I'd be jailed, not for Actual Bodily Harm and it being my first offence.

Wowee, thanks a bundle, I already knew that. So what does that tell you? That cases and verdicts had nothing to do with justice, only on some cantankerous old twat thinking he had to dish it out at least once a day regardless? **Fucking charming**.

When I stood in front of the three male Magistrates this time, my hopes rose for a tick - as in half of tick tock, it was that quick - the man on the right was black. Now I wasn't expecting 'Respect to yor, white brother' but I did think he might have had a bit of sympathy for my struggle, seeing as the NF was sort of involved. Just my luck though, he was even sterner than Staedtler and Waldorf sitting up there with him. According to 'Mister' Cockram's statement (he wasn't in court), I'd threatened him on the bus home, had followed him to the curry house and had shouted threats and obscenities at him. And I'd commenced a completely unprovoked attack on him. Yeah right, tell us another one, Jackanory. *'Mister' Lying Bastard* more like. I did attempt a protest for a second but the bastard barked at me to shut up before I could complete the word 'but'. I shook my head in hurt disbelief and looked at the floor. The fact that Cockram had suffered swollen cheekbone, black eyes, cut lip and a cauliflower ear didn't exactly help my cause, I must admit. He carried on in his sneering posh voice but most of what he said went in one ear, took a short jaunt across my mind and sailed out of the other. I do remember him saying that no one had the right to use violence to express their political beliefs and that drunkenness was no excuse. It's a good job I forgot his name, otherwise there would've been no excuse for me making abusive phone calls and sending parcels of dog shit to him in the post, either. When it finally came to it, I pleaded guilty as instructed by Sugar, 'For the best'. The Magistrate finished with saying I should be thoroughly ashamed of myself and that he never wanted to see me in a court of law again. Like I wanted to see him again, anywhere, the tosser. He'd *loved* it, specially when he slapped me with a two hundred quid fine and bound me over to keep the peace for two years. Every cloud and all that shit though, at least it wasn't reported in the Evening Post and the bloke at the DSS told me not to mention it on any job applications. My mum went halves on the fine too, which was brilliant of her. We sent them a two quid cheque every week, it was just like doing the Kay's catalogue except all I got was a record and an ill fitting crown. I had to pay the thirty-three quid for the dentist myself though, my mum wasn't totally on my side. You'd have thought I'd learned my lesson but I saw Cockram in town a few days later at a bus stop on Vicar Lane. I felt like having another go at him there and then, except it was daylight and there were loads of people milling about. Instead, I just smiled at him and he shat himself.

Most blokes are guilty of one sexual offence or another. Okay, it might only be a sly pinch of a girl's bum in a nightclub or in the office but it's still an offence. Anyway, I'm on about the more serious stuff, like attempted rape, not just messing about. Look at your average lad, a virgin so desperate to break his duck that the piggy bank in his bedroom could expect a break in to fund the services of a certain kind of lady. He'll try his hardest to get his paws on his girlfriend - if he's actually got one - to score maximum flesh points and to enter the world of sexual adulthood. Until that is, he hears 'No, stop it' in his ear and feels her restraining grip on his wandering hands. And then he'll give up . . . for a few seconds anyway, before another manoeuvre, another angle of attack is commenced. It'll carry on like that, he'll keep trying, ferreting away at the girl's defences like a... well like a ferret, until he gets a result. The *result* could be one from a few, like a slap in the face and her storming off, or a fondle of her breasts and a swift tweak of her nipples. Even better would be a fumble down in her knickers.

The reason I know men are guilty is because I have been said beast in that same identity parade. When a teenage lad is randy (like, when isn't he?), he's a dog on heat, he really is. Alright, the tongue doesn't hang out as much and the toilet training is a bit better but the desperate look and the lack of ethics is the same. And there comes a time when a hundred daily tugs isn't satisfying enough, even with a portfolio of muff around your feet or even a tasty video to watch. So when the lad finally gets his hands on a girl, self-control and gentlemanly conduct fly out of the window. Hands everywhere, furiously kissing, forcing his tongue into her mouth, lovebites, grappling, overpowering her protests, ripping at her clothes, fiddling with her bra strap to liberate her loveliness. And not forgetting the thrusting of his groin so she's in **no doubt** as to the size of his desire. And all of this could be in the first minute: sexual experience is buried treasure for boys. In his head, it's the time when 'no' really means 'yes', of that he has little doubt. She can't resist him but she has to *say* *it* to try and prove she's not really *that* kind of girl. She's gagging for it as much as he is. If she says no again, she still doesn't mean it, she *is* proving she isn't that kind of girl and yet she's powerless to his charms and her own desires. Any more than two or three 'no's and there's something wrong (with her) and he'd better cool down before he gets into trouble.

The problem is, he doesn't, he *can't*. He's got this far, he needs satisfaction, his body yearns for it - he's got a hard on throbbing so much his balls ache. Whatever's going on in her head, he prays she'll open up for another chance. He'd do or promise virtually anything to get his way with her. I'd had a few such battles of my own with girls at house parties and in 'clubs and town alleyways but I'd remained a sad virgin. At least I listened to the sensible, decent voice in my head and never forced things too far. What would have happened without that voice, I'm glad I never found out. When I did break my duck, lose my cherry, my virginity, whatever you want to call it, it was all so easy. I wondered why I'd worried so much, why I'd made so many crusty bits on my sheets; all those restless hours in bed I'd spent, tossing and tossing, thinking that a shag was the most important thing in life.

It's great being a bloke - you can go out and shag till your dick drops off and all you'll get is 'What a lad, what a pulling machine' and 'Good on him, he's playing the field, sowing his oats, it's natural'. But if a woman does it, fuck me, she's a slag, she's a tart, a whore, a slut, the town bike, *you name it*. I met Suzie in Martine's, the shithole 'club near the Corn Exchange. The place shouldn't have been that bad actually, the building itself was nice enough and the music okay, but it's the quality of customers that make or break nightspots. Martine's was all gum and beer sticky carpets, a broken glass coated dance floor and piss and puke flooded toilets - and that was just the ladies - so I never expected to meet a princess there. I usually had to be rat-arsed to chat women up but I was lucky with Suzie, she was sitting on her own near the dance floor and I had enough bottle to plonk myself next to her without being out of my tree at that stage. I was sure she'd been eyeing me up (you **are** with a gallon inside you - Dutch courage is a brilliant import). I waded in with a smile and 'Hello' and an early 'I think you're lovely' and we were soon necking away. I sneakily stroked her breasts hoping no one could see and she rubbed my knob in return, making an explosion in my trousers likely. It was lavish, it always is when a woman isn't backward in coming forward and there are few better feelings than a woman wanting you. We had a smooch to Spandau Ballet and I could tell she was impressed with my constant hard on, I was just glad I'd not shot in my pants. She invited me back to her house in Halton Moor and insisted on paying for the taxi, I wasn't going to argue. I was relieved she had her own place, I was screwed staying at my mum's and for God's sake, they might even have been friends at school for all I knew. We sat in her living room over hot small talk and coffee. I was desperate to get her upstairs, not only for the obvious but now because my sober eye was slowly re-focusing and Suzie was becoming less attractive and more in girth than I'd first thought. I made my way upstairs and undressed in her bedroom while she locked up. I slipped in to her unmade bed, shaking and shivering, though it wasn't cold.

Her tits looked better when she had her clothes on - they were wider and saggier in the flesh - and her nipples were tiny, like Jelly Tots but nowhere near as nice. And she was a bit dry down below which was not a pleasant thing to find out: it wasn't meant to be like that. It all went much quicker than I'd hoped for (and her no doubt) and my love commando had soon disobeyed orders. When I finally managed to get inside her - she had to put it up for me, I couldn't even find her hole properly - I was off like 'the clappers'. She told me to slow down but it was already too late, I'd already come. I tried to continue with a semi on but my heart wasn't in it and she was far from impressed, I was sober enough to work that one out. She tutted and turned her back on me to sleep. I wanted to tell her to wait as I'd soon be ready to have another go. I *needed* to, she wouldn't have regretted it, but I'd blown it. After a sly attempt at discovering her body properly - unfortunately, her arms were crossed and legs shut tight - I slid out of bed and dressed. I crept down the stairs and tried ringing for a taxi but her phone was cut off. I took some shrapnel from her purse for a phone box - I could've nicked more but that crap's out of order - and walked to York Road with my head high and shoulders broad. It was early morning freezing fog with no one around to see my proud swagger.

I met the lads the night after in the Blooming Rose down Hunslet. It was a great feeling, like I'd scored the winner in a match. They were patting me on the back and buying me drinks and hardly stopped asking me about it. I told them that me and Suzie had been at it like rabbits all night, that she was gagging for it and that she had beautiful firm tits, nipples like chapel hatpegs and a very tidy arse, thank you. The fact that a couple of them must have known she looked nothing like that didn't seem to matter: it was official, I was now a man. Only I wasn't man enough to admit how poor my sexual debut had been.

We always drank in the proper pubs in town on Friday and Saturday nights, those with tap rooms and hand-pulled Tetley's like the Horse and Trumpet. The beer was cheap and the jukebox only five pee a play with loads of Stranglers, Cure, New Order and Joy Div on it. It had the worst bogs in Leeds though; you had to go outside the back and across a little cobbled yard past crates and barrels to get to them. They were like from Queen Victoria's day, serious, and it was always brass monkeys, even in summer. I thought that was the reason for the burning every time I had a slash, like the stinging I sometimes got as a boy, but it soon grew in to pissing razors. I started waking up in the night hoping it was a bad dream. It wasn't. Eventually I didn't even have to pee for it to hurt and my knob started to smell rancid. In private I'd slip my hand down my kegs and sniff my fingers to see if the tell tale tail smell was still there. It was, the fucking thing wouldn't go away. The worst thing was that I couldn't talk to anyone about it, the lads would rip the piss out of me and I couldn't trust even Gaz to keep his gob shut. I wished I'd never met the old slag, she must have known she had something wrong with her. I hated her for it - the scabby witch Suzie, a social diseased pillow of society - I couldn't fathom how anyone could be so cruel. I wondered how many other poor saps she'd infected with her poison.

A few days went by and I was getting more and more worried, my stomach was lurching all the time and I felt like crying. I had to do something before my poorly cock started to rot away - and it was never big enough as it was. I once read about Al Capone dying of syphilis and I remember photos of kids being deformed when they were born because their mums had it when they were pregnant. **Fucking hell**. Then I thought of someone who'd sort it out - Doctor Baxter, he'd been our doctor forever, since I was a twinkle in my parents' mince pies. I cursed myself for not thinking of him before. I left home the next morning in plenty of time but walked straight past the Old Lane Surgery. How could I tell him that I'd got a dose from a woman my mum's age? And what if he told her? I'd be screwed, that's what - kicked out of the house on my arse and disowned as the Bottomley Leper. I went to Tait's paper shop on Dews Road. I hope no one saw me because I must have looked a right tit, scouring the problem pages in women's magazines.

I slammed the phone down twice before I asking for help from a woman at the Samaritans. She was dead nice when I eventually got the words out. She told me which ward to go to in Leeds General Infirmary and even directions inside because it's massive. I went on the Monday morning, my signing on day, to save on bus fares. I couldn't stop thinking about something called the umbrella I'd heard the lads talk of - the doctors rammed it down your dick and it was absolute agony. I hoped, *prayed,* it was a myth. I got to the hospital just before nine, thinking it'd be quiet. I was way off the mark with that one, Jesus: the big corridor she'd told me about was heaving, with hospital staff and patients everywhere. I found Ward 12 easy enough, it was one of loads of pale green doors, with 'Special Clinic' printed on it. Shakin Stevens' 'Green Door' began to play in my head, over and over, the talentless bastard. *'Behind the green doo-OR.'*

I dived in, hoping no one saw me, and followed the sign for the Men's Ward. It was boiling and smelt of antiseptic, reminding me of getting smacked at West Brom when the coach driver had cleaned my face up of blood. A woman sitting at a desk, older than I'd expected and looking more like a pen pusher than a nurse, looked up at me; there was no way out now. She took my name and address and stuff and then asked me how I'd got the infection - who with, when and where and if I'd had sexual relations with anyone else since. It was calm and polite and she seemed sympathetic more than anything else, I'd expected a bollocking or a lecture. I **had** hoped for a fella, with us talking like blokes do, 'Well it was like this mate, I pulled this bird in Martine's who liked me having a hard on when we were smooching' and him grinning and nodding knowingly, almost in envy. She even asked me if I could tell the woman to go in for treatment, because they don't always know they've got anything up with them. I thought sod that for a game of soldiers, if I saw her again I'd more likely give her what she deserved, a slap; I wasn't going to put myself for her. I told the nurse it'd happened at a party but of course I'd tell her if I saw her. She told me to go sit in the waiting room around the corner. There were four blokes already there, two sitting next to each other in the front row and two others separate. I didn't like the look of the two together, with tattoos all over them, even on their necks. They both sniggered when they saw me so I sat at the back, blushing like an infant. I sat and waited, crapping myself and hoping it'd all be over with quick. I kept on punishing myself for not using a contraceptive. The tattooed blokes snapped me out of my sorry state, being dead loud, mouthing off and laughing about women they'd pulled and what diseases they'd caught. It was as if they were playing Social Disease Bingo, trying to get a full house or something. Shoot me if I'm ever that low.

A younger nurse led me to a curtained cubicle. She was pleasant and treated me like a normal person, not a dirty little toerag which let's face it, I was. She wasn't bad looking either, though a bit chubby. Not that I took too much notice, pulling the opposite sex wasn't a high priority at the time. She took a drop of blood from my arm and then I had to give a urine sample in the bog which wasn't easy, holding a jug in one hand and aiming in to it with my stricken dick in the other. Surprise surprise, I peed on my hand and splashed the floor. I wiped it up with loo roll, more than the tattooed tossers would have done, I was sure. When I got back to my chair one of them was being led to a side room and he wasn't laughing or being a big man now. To my embarrassment, or *more* to my embarrassment should I say, I couldn't stop wondering if he had tattoos on his tackle. I'm not sure if I felt better or worse - it would be my turn soon, very soon. Another side door opened and an Asian doctor in a white overcoat stepped out. Even though I was watching him it still made me jump when he called my name out. I half expected someone to laugh when he pronounced it 'Bottom-lee' but no one said a dicky bird. It felt like a long walk.

Inside, he told me he was Doctor Patel and asked me about the symptoms. Then he asked if I'd had oral sex with the woman. *No, why, should I have?* I'm glad I hadn't or I could've been in even deeper shit: I never knew you could get infected in your mouth and on your tongue. Jesus, imagine that, imagine what your food would taste of **every** time you ate something. I went behind the screen and took my jeans off while he wheeled in a squeaky trolley with a tray of weird looking surgical instruments on. I purposely looked away from it. He prepared himself, stretching on a pair of see-through gloves and told me to pull down the front of my Y-fronts and hold my penis out, foreskin pulled back. I felt so hot and dirty and ashamed that I was burning and my scalp itched with heat. He told me what he was going to do with one instrument and then the second and that there might be a little pain. I kept quiet, I don't think I was able to say anything, I was so dry. He bent down and slowly inserted a swab down my knob 'eye'. It stung. Then he sort of twisted it and scraped me inside, it stung even more, and he pulled it out which felt ten times as bad, like he'd cut me. My eyes were watering and I could feel trickles of sweat rolling down my back. I shuddered for a second. I tried to go in to a trance to blank it all out, like at the dentist, but I failed. He tinkered around on the tray. I couldn't stop myself looking down. I nearly shat myself when I saw what he was aiming at my dick with: a thin little metal rod with a circle of four or five tiny spikes pointing up the stem. It was the umbrella the lads had talked about. I tried to take a deep breath but there was no air and I felt dizzy and my legs trembled like mad. He pushed it in again and it made the throbbing sharper. Then he pushed it in further. ***For fuck's sake it couldn't go any further.*** I was positive he'd gone too deep in the most sensitive part you can think of, ever. A dentist's drill was piss easy compared to this, believe me. But then he slid it out saying he was finished and the throbbing cooled and slowed. I couldn't believe there was no blood. I nearly started roaring I was that relieved it was all over with. I muttered a thank you while I got dressed and he left the room with me sweating like a pig, struggling to get into my jeans. He came back a couple of minutes later and told me I had non-specific urethritis, NSU for short, and gave me a small bottle of antibiotics which would clear it up in about ten days. I couldn't drink any alcohol in that time. Heartbreaking, I don't think. I felt like hugging every nurse I saw as I left the hospital. *'Behind the green doo-OR!'*

It was three weeks before I went out with the lads. I told them I'd had tonsillitis again, which was sort of true as I did get it every now and then. The drizzle made town quiet that Friday night - Leeds people never like getting their hair wet. The lads decided to go for an Indian at Drifters at about half ten. I love curries but I wouldn't eat in that hole, you couldn't be sure what you were getting, seagulls and dogs and shit. And the stairs in there were a health hazard on their own. I left them to it and walked towards the Corn Exchange bus stop. I was still thirsty and still felt good; I was clean now and my fresh rubber johnnies were burning a hole in my pocket. Who knew, I might get lucky? The nearest club was Martine's so my resolution of never going there again failed within weeks. I persuaded the bouncers I was old enough to get in and got a pint of electric bitter and leant back on the bar, feet sticking to the carpet, scouring the dark for girls. It was mostly men and the few skirts that *were* there didn't want to know. With no one to talk to, gravelled glass ruining my brogues and bleeding Spandau Ballet blaring out made me realise how lonely it was, how lonely *I* was. I vowed never to go to a nightclub on my own again, never mind there. I drained my pint, deciding to cut my losses and catch the Nightrider. And then I recognized Suzie at the end of the bar. You'd never think she was thirty-eight, she looked like a twenty year old, albeit a big twenty year old. If I'd thought about it properly I should have still left but it was Friday night and you need things to happen on Friday nights. I bought another pint and went over to talk to her. I wanted to be nice and tell her about the hospital and *maybe* even pull her again.

When I said hello she said, 'Who are you?' in a tone that actually said 'Who *the fuck* are you ?'.

What a bitch. I felt that big I tell you. I couldn't believe she could be like that after all she'd put me through. I turned away and thought bollocks to her, let her die of her mot rot. I walked to the gents, noticing my reflection in a big new shiny Durex machine on the wall inside. You have to laugh.

I must admit whilst I was aiming at the pineapple chunks in the piss tray I thought I'd been a bit hard on her - maybe she hadn't known she had an infection, like the nurse had suggested. And maybe she really didn't remember me, though she was a cow anyway, no mistaking. If I didn't tell her about the VD then I'd be the villain and I wasn't going to have that. So I went back to the bar to sort it out. She was talking to another man and when she saw me I saw her say something to him straight away, probably along the lines of 'There's that little shit who was pestering me'. Whatever it was, he turned around and gave me real daggers. I don't know which made me feel worse, him wanting to kick ten bags of shit out of me or the tattoos I recognised on his neck. I looked away sharpish and fled.

I've never seen Suzie since and I've not been in Martine's either. I'm glad. She's probably popped her clogs the same way Al Capone did and it might just serve her right. If I'm honest though, I'm sort of grateful: thanks to her I grew up in more ways than one.

I was one of the first punks to appear in Leeds when it splattered on to our music scene. It's easy to say it but it's a total lie. Actually, I missed the boat, sort of on purpose, and I waited for the next less shocking one to come along. While I knew lads like Tigger, Nut and Dev were down our street embarking on spiking and dying their hair, wearing mental clothes and pogo-spitting for England, I was safe at home playing Beatles records with the headphones on, or watching the anaesthetised Top of the Pops.

Whilst I didn't have the guts for rebels' clothing, I wasn't completely dormant inside, I knew what the deejays were preaching about the Brotherhood of Man, Boney M and others of similar 'calibre' being great talents was utter shite and I was sick of the soulless disco slop and long haired saps with socks stuffed down their kegs playing their twenty minute guitar solos. The music scene needed a rocket up its arse, something new and refreshing, and it got one; a kick in the bollocks to be more accurate.

All the arguments about where punk originated, was it here with Malcolm McLaren and the Sex Pistols, or was it in America with The New York Dolls, who gives a shit, really? And what did punk stand for? Anarchy, antiestablishment, fighting mods/rockers/skinheads/ each other, sniffing glue, telling everyone to 'Fuck off, leave me alone' or staying in bed all day, it all stood for different things to different people. I wondered if punk had brought these attitudes out or would they have appeared anyway. I mean, life wasn't exactly pleasant in the seventies as it was, plenty of people were pissed off aplenty, whether it was unemployment, strikes, unions, low pay, the government, trouble on the terraces, inflation or the Jubilee or flares and platform shoes (naturally), there was always *something*, and the bad feeling and social discontent infected my age group more than any other. These bands were original and fresh and *did* make you feel like getting off your arse to do what you wanted to do, not what *they* wanted you to do. The new wave weren't always great musicians or great singing voices but they had an energy and creativity that put most of the rest to shame. As with anything new and quality, there was a lot of dross that jumped on the bandwagon with it but most punk and new wave music - or whatever they needed to class it as - was exciting, and when was the last time you could say that? Before most of us were born, that's when.

Typical of me then though, I was scared to look different, I didn't want to be beaten up in the street or have abuse hurled at me, I was happy enough being seen as a regular clothes wearing, neatly combed side-parting **normal** sort of chap. I did get my hair spiked and wear black and white striped drainpipes for a short time, when it was no longer too different, and I looked a right prick.

Punk and new wave eventually became trendy, it wasn't about 'fighting the system' any more, being independent or giving two fingered salutes to authority, it was about selling more records, fashion and merchandise. It was all a massive contradiction. I don't believe Johnny Rotten expected the Sex Pistols to get as popular as they did, and they'd become what he'd set out for them not to be - predictable and commercial - and to be fair to him, he left before they really sold out with the film and the embarrassing singles and gimmicks. Punks in the street dwindled and were slowly replaced by clones in all black with long spikey dyed-black hair, layers of ghostly make up and lots of pseudo Gothic jewellery. We christened them the fashion punks, they were an embarrassment, all trying to be so different, and all looking so alike.

I bought and stole tons of singles, black vinyl or lovely coloured ones, and I treasure them and never got shut of them. Bands like The Pistols and The Damned and The Ruts and The Buzzcocks and The Undertones and The Dead Kennedys and Siouxsie & The Banshees, and loads more. Most of the groups seemed to vanish or fade away, though their music and its impact never did. My favourites were always The Stranglers, four malevolent looking men dressed in black. They arrived in the charts roughly at the same time as punk and forever had to live being branded the same, but they were never that, they were much much more. For a start off, they sounded totally original and their music always consisted of brilliant different styles; you could never categorize them. Some people said that they sounded like The Doors or The Seeds. No way was that right, they sounded nothing like The Doors except that both groups had a fantastic keyboardist and who's ever heard of The Seeds? And The Stranglers were great musicians, they could actually sing and none of them had spiky hair, just spiky attitudes. They wrote controversial songs and were always creating trouble for themselves, treating journalists like dirt (nothing wrong with that, in my book) and basically being antisocial most of the time. They weren't particularly pleasant to their fans either, aggressive and cold on stage, but we knew it was just a front. Not that a front was needed, I always thought them tough anyway, with athletic and muscular Jean Jacques Burnel on bass, a genuine Doc Mart wearing karate expert, and the bulky drummer Jet Black with his beard and scowl looking like a cross between a Hell's Angel and a seriously aggrieved bouncer, and wiry, wily Hugh Cornwell on lead and main vocals who'd rip you apart with his piss taking, never mind the look of someone who might easily set about you with a flick knife any time. The exception was Dave Greenfield on keyboards, who with his long dark hair and tash looked like a mad wizard. He *was* a wizard, you could shove your Rick Wakemans and Vangelises and bloody Elton Johns, Dave Greenfield was the best keyboard player ever.

The Stranglers were misogynists, women haters, their lyrics proved it, according to the journalists. Yeah, they wrote violent and insulting stuff but so what, it didn't mean they were *anything*. Their LP La Folie (which HMV had kindly donated to the Bottomley cause that time), the lyrics were all about love, the selfishness and falseness of it, not about hating women. The Raven LP, shamefully overlooked or underrated, was political if anything, and didn't just refer to the state of Britain. Their infamous top ten single Peaches was about fellas on the beach getting turned on by sexy women in bikinis, that was all. Sod it, it didn't matter to me what they sang about, as long as they weren't supporting nazis or Tories, it was their music I loved.

The normal format for a group is singer, lead guitar, bass guitar and drums, and sometimes extras like synthesizer, rhythm guitar and even brass instruments. With The Stranglers, you regularly got the *bass* as the distinctive lead sound, and a choice of two great singers in

Cornwell and Burnel. And Greenfield's keyboard playing was totally out in a league of its own. Not only did they come out with vibrant, energetic, sinister songs, they had lovely 'ballads' and waltzes up their sleeves in abundance. I saw them about twenty times, not bad I suppose but pathetic compared to other fans, like my mate Turtle, who I met through the concerts. He saw them easy a hundred times. Fair's fair, I could never afford that many gigs and I liked my home comforts too much to travel rough across the country. It made no odds to me anyway, it's what you feel inside about something that counts - brilliant if you can prove it by following them all around the shop but not essential - and I loved 'The Meninblack' just like I loved Leeds United.

I met Jean Jacques Burnel ('JJ') once, when he was signing autographs in HMV in town. There was about a hundred people there, and I queued for an hour to see him. He was sitting behind the counter, signing whatever people had brought in for him to sign - no women's tits or bums unfortunately - and I had an armful of singles and albums at the ready. He wasn't the scowling, threatening karate kicker we saw on stage, he was a smiling, polite and friendly bloke. I was getting more nervous as I neared the front and my heart was pounding, as if I was about to take a penalty in a big match or be penalised in court.

'Alright mate?' he said, in a soft London twang. 'Do you want them signing?' looking at my offerings.

'Yes please, JJ,' I replied. At least I'd managed to say *something* though my original in depth questions such as, 'You know on 'European Female' - where you sing superbly incidentally - I read that there's five languages used, but I can only find four, what's the other?' or 'Do you remember kicking my mate Turtle in the bollocks backstage, that time in Manchester?' completely disappeared.

'Whose name shall I put it for?'

'Mine. Steve ... Steve Bottomley.'

He chuckled, 'Bottomley? There's an unfortunate name.'

'Don't take the piss out of my name, JJ, please!'

'Just pulling your leg, mate. How can I take the piss with a name like mine?'

I said, 'True' but I always thought his name was dead cool.

'What would you like me to write?' he asked.

I thought for a moment and then blurted, 'I don't know, summat dead deep, that could change my life?' *Fucking hell, where did I get that one from?* 'Sorry, I'm just a bit nervous.'

'*You're* nervous?'

He wasn't serious, surely.

Now *he* thought for a moment, the concentration on his face belying his boyish and tough features. He wrote words in silver ink on the Raven album cover and put it to one side to start signing the rest of my offerings. He finished and offered his hand - *he* offered to shake *my* hand - and we did, a good, firm handshake. I walked away, smiling, still shaking slightly, now sweating, with his farewell, 'You take care Steve, and just be yourself,' echoing in my head.

The opening line JJ Burnel sings on the song 'The Raven' is, 'Fly straight, with perfection...' and that's what he'd written on the record sleeve.

Leeds United is my team - slice me open and you'd see LUFC carved on my heart - but I'd never really been your typical football supporter, I've never hated everyone else, you see. In fact, I quite liked some of the other English teams, especially when they were winning trophies in Europe. That didn't include Man United naturally ('Scum'), who won sod all, anyway, and I hated the Germans, Bayern Munich for obvious reasons, and Bob Stokoe, the manager of Sunderland. I'd hated him since they beat us in 1973 in the FA Cup Final and he'd danced around Wembley like a vainglorious saviour, without sparing a thought for the losers. *And* he'd slagged Don Revie off, for years. Sunderland actually played very well and deserved to win the match but Stokoe wasn't in the same league as The Don.

The four floodlights on the corners of the Elland Road football ground were brilliant. They made the Leeds United stadium famous and were a source of genuine pride for not only Beeston people but all of us in the city. The tallest in Europe, maybe even the world, they were proper feats of engineering: four manmade shining diamonds high in the South Leeds sky. I grew up with them and they were a part of me, always there, constants. In daylight, you could see them from miles away and the city was recognizable because of them. And at night - well, *Jesus* - you could read your local newspaper by them, whichever Northern satellite town you were in at the time. The floodlights were a genuine landmark and how many people could boast about having such a thing in their neighbourhood?

Until the people in charge, probably the council, decided to pull them down, and make it into another ordinary English football ground. Now it had joined the rest - nothing original, nothing special - and why? Was the city of Leeds running short of bleeding cutlery or something, or were local scrap metal dealers giving the bosses of the club and the council tidy little backhanders?

You can tell how badly a team's doing by the drop in crowds and the songs the surviving supporters sing. You won't hear 'We're gonna win the League' when their team is propping up the league table, obviously, what you will hear is, 'You're gonna get your fucking heads kicked in' every time an opposing team scores, and similar warm hearted ditties. 'Bastard, bastard, bastard' was my particular favourite, on the rare occasion it cropped up. With all the time, money and effort spent following a team, only to see them play shite and players not give a shit, the mood of the crowd is bound to get worse. Leeds were in Division Two then and though they weren't bottom, they were performing with the potential to get there, even with the old master Eddie Gray playing and managing. To make things worse, every team from Barnsley to Shrewsbury was desperate to beat the ex-kings of Europe, and often played the games of their lives. I honestly never even knew where bloody Shrewsbury was before.

The night Arsenal came to Elland Road, with Rix and other great players like Liam Brady and Pat Jennings, was a break from the normal grind for us as it was a Cup replay. If we won, maybe the good times weren't too far away. I mean, if we could beat First Division Arsenal then we could beat anyone, it stood to reason. I'd never seen Leeds win owt since my Dad died and I craved success so much I ached inside, I really did.

We played well. We even took an extra time lead through Aidan Butterworth who could hardly stand he was so knackered. It was so near the end of the match, Wembley wasn't such a daft distant dream after all. But then Arsenal got a free kick, miles out. Rix took it. He hit this ridiculous harmless looking curling shot - which very possibly might not even have been a shot - which took John Lukic by surprise. Lukic was a great 'keeper but he couldn't half be gormless at times (worse than the Scouse christened 'Careless Hands' Sprakey) and this was one of those times. The ball bounced in front of him then, sneaking just inside his right-hand post, hit the net. Arsenal had equalized and their players and fans went mental. Great gasps of disappointment were all we could manage we were that stunned. We couldn't even muster a choral threat to rearrange their boat races. We'd blown it, yet another team had pissed on our bonfire. After the final whistle I stood with Gaz on the Kop terrace for a while, hunched over a barrier, wondering how we'd let the team fool us into believing they were good again.

We trudged out with a few fellow disbelievers, hardly speaking, and walked towards the main gates to go home. As we passed the players' entrance underneath the West Stand, who should come out but the geeky looking, silly blond permed Graham Rix. I actually thought of sportingly congratulating him but I didn't get chance as this thirtyish fat, greasy haired bloke in anorak and red and white scarf scampered up to him.

'Grime, you wus brilliant, triffic! Soin us this will ya, mite' which in proper English I think translated to, 'Graham, you were brilliant, terrific' and a request for his autograph.

Now I had nothing against this kind of man normally, the sort that lives, breathes and probably self-abuses over football but this guy was too much. Who did he think he was, coming here with his accent, broadcasting his love for the team who'd just spawned a draw against us? Fair enough, away supporters should be allowed to visit but you don't take the piss out of the wallpaper or tread mud in on the carpet when you're a guest. Gaz walked on, I stopped to watch the Arsenal fella's nose get browner and browner while he adored his hero, and I decided appropriate action was needed, a necessary lesson. I put to the back of my red-misted mind the fact that I was bound over by the law to keep the peace, this struck me as being more important. We walked through the gates to wait across the road where Big Jack Charlton used to sell from his souvenir stall before matches. There were other people waiting around in gloomy doorways and shadows an' all, and a few coppers on overtime, spending time over sod all except sending people on their way. The anoracked Cockney emerged through the gates and turned left on to Elland Road.

I strode over to catch up with him. I growled, 'This is for Graham Rix you Cockney prick. Piss off back to the hole you came from'. He was surprised and as he looked at me I punched him in the face, and again. I must admit, his reaction - a high pitched yelp of fear more than pain - shamed me, the poor bastard. But he shouldn't have been there, he should have been rolling out the barrel down the Old Kent Road, eating jellied eels and having a 'larf' with Pearly Kings and Queens, not up North in the real world with whippets, dole and mashed tea. Suddenly, I heard shouts and people running.

Gaz called, 'Watch it, Steve' so I ran, pelted past the burger van in front of The Peacock car park, glimpsing the woman lean out, yelling, 'You're all the same you lot, spoiling it for the rest ...'

I carried on running and snorted a 'Get stuffed' at her over my shoulder, up Wesley Street I went and through a snicket on to the old quarry, slowing to walking pace. There was a group of men standing around as if they were waiting for something. I couldn't make out their faces even though the floodlights were illuminating most of South Leeds.

'Been chased?' one of them asked me, not in a London accent which was a relief.

'Yeah, only by coppers though. I lost 'em'.

'What fo'?'

'Oh I smacked this Cockney, he was pissing me off.'

'Good lad. Are you here on Saturday, why don't you meet up with us in the Templar before, for a few pints?' and that was it. I didn't know their names, what they looked like even or why they were there but I did feel this was an important invitation.

I hate it when people are jolly, especially when it's my mum, **more** especially when I'm suffering from a clanging hangover, which is what I was doing this particular Saturday morning. She wasn't just being jolly, she was taking the piss, like she'd got me a surprise present or had some *smashing* news for me. She was being a giddy kipper, to use one of her favourite expressions, and I was being a narky old trout.

She nearly sang it, 'There was a telephone call for you last night, just after you'd gone out'.

'Oh yeah, one of the lads?' I asked, probably grumpily.

'Ooooh no!'

For fuck's sake Mother, stop fucking about and tell me what you're fucking well on about. I didn't say that, I just thought it. 'Who then?' definitely grumpily.

'A girl. Andrea. And she *really* likes you, I can tell. Will you call her?' and she passed me a scratty piece of paper with Andrea written on it, complete with three exclamation marks and a telephone number. Had she known what this Andrea was really like, I don't think she'd've been so chirpy. At least now any suspicions she might've had about her eldest son lifting shirts were out of the window.

I'd suffered from a single lad's nightmare: I'd gone through a soul destroying lean patch, pulling wise. In other words, I'd not had a shag for months, since losing my virginity in fact, *not even a sniff*. Mike, Gaz's elder brother, called it a veritable drought. He often used words none of us were sure about and he'd get the piss took out of him for doing it. Not that it's important but on the quiet I used to ask him what the words meant. Regards the telephone message, the week before, I'd been out on the town with the lads as usual and we'd ended up in the downstairs of Cullens, a little wine bar near the Hotel Metropole. When we walked in, we were wolf whistled by a group of women seated around a table near the door. I didn't think I'd be one of the lucky targets but I looked over to them anyway, as you do, hoping but not showing it, and a pretty dark haired lass with lovely blue eyes stared right back at me. She winked and I did a double-take, making her laugh. Now I didn't bottle it, but I wasn't exactly Allan Wells off the mark to go over and talk to her, either. It's true about the walk over to a bird you fancy being a bloody long one, I was nervous as hell. Luckily for me though, Desperate Dave had got the nod off the lass who'd whistled, a big curly haired blonde with huge norks and he dragged me over with him. The others, Mike, Gaz and Wince, went to play pool in the back room, so if I didn't pull now, there was only me to blame. Me and the dark haired lass got chatting and it was nice, we were getting on alright. Then the next thing I know Dave and the blonde are swapping spit for England. It didn't happen like that normally, if one of the lads ever pulled it was in a 'club, never a pub or bar. Maybe it's with nightclubs being darker I don't know, as people can't see who they're fondling or playing tonsil hockey with. Anyway, the other lasses carried on gabbing as if nothing had happened but I was a bit embarrassed, and jealous to be honest, like a giftless kid at a party.

'Why aren't we doing that?' I asked.

'We can if you like ... outside,' she replied.

We left Dave and the blonde tongue-tied and the others with jaws snippier than a hairdresser's scissors.

Cullens is off the beaten track in town, it's more businesses and solicitors' offices than anything and so it's usually dead quiet on a night. We walked arm in arm through the streets for a while and came across Park Square. We couldn't have picked a better place if we'd tried - it's pleasant, small and peaceful, with park benches, flowerbeds and ornamental fences making it pretty even in the dark. We sat on a bench and kissed passionately, tongues down each other's throat like we'd been at it for years. Lovely, she was a great kisser, and I had a raging hard on right away (no great change there then). She let me stroke and squeeze her breasts which were brilliantly firm and she was rubbing my dick, it was great (too great in fact, I had to pull her hand away, I wanted to impress her later). I slowly stroked my hand up her skirt, fingers soon inside her legs, rubbing her warmth through her lace knickers.

I thought she was loving it, she was breathing heavily, but she said, 'No, not here' and I thought **bollocks**, I'd blown it. She went to sit on the grass behind the bench and said 'Here'. I nearly shot my load there and then, I tell you. She laid back as I sat down next to her and it wasn't long before I'd pulled her knickers down - is there anything sexier? I lay on top of her, positioning myself between her legs, pressing myself against her. And then we were necking again and I was fumbling and then fingering her and she becoming wetter and wetter, it was beautiful. She was grappling with my belt and unzipping me. I asked her if she wanted me to use anything for protection. She scolded me for thinking I'd catch something. I didn't argue, I wasn't exactly gonna say 'I think I should warn you miss, I have only recently recovered from a sexually transmitted disease' was I? I managed to slip into her unaided and it was a fantastic feeling of warm and wetness. She gasped, more music to my ears. That and her moans of pleasure were sending me but I kept the urge to 'sprint home' pretty well in check, pumping as slowly and steadily as I could.

'Nice 'n' Sleazy does it.'

I still didn't last very long. That's the trouble, the more she toys with your truncheon, the less actual *damage* you can do with it. And I was still a relative newcomer. Not that she complained, specially as I told her I'd soon get a hard on again. We screwed twice more and it was ace, the last time with her on top. She was the best I'd had, no danger. Let's face it, she was only my second and she couldn't have been worse than the first, with or without the dose of VD I'd taken away with me as a memento. I would've asked to see her again but she'd told me she had a two year old son and so, for me, that was it, I didn't want any baggage involvement. Okay, I knew I'd just used her (*she'd* used me, too) but I didn't want to *carry on* using her. I'd not gone out that night with the intention of having a one night stand, no matter what it might look like. There was a battle going on in my head: lust versus decency, and the more beer I got in me the more lust prevailed and the more indecent I got. And on top of that, when a woman comes on to you, an erect penis has no conscience. I didn't know what to do - I didn't want to hurt her feelings but I sure didn't want her hurting mine in the future, either. I took the coward's way out and kept my frequent feelings of loneliness to myself and my mouth firmly shut. Anyway, her being twenty-five and me not yet eighteen was far too big a gap, as it was. I didn't want a Ready Made Family, it wouldn't be fair on her or the sprog, never mind me. Good luck to blokes that do, it was just something I couldn't take on or even consider. I put her in a taxi to Cross Gates and said I'd see her around. Even though I did feel guilty, I enjoyed telling the lads about my exploits, and what with Dave's tales an' all, it had been a bloody good night. It turns out that he and the blonde (he called her a blonde bombshell, we called her the Blonde Bombsite) ended up shagging in a phone box in City Square. I couldn't believe it. I mean, a phone box, and it's dead bright in City Square, somebody must've seen them at it, talk about lack of class.

I don't remember giving her my address nor my phone number but she had them anyhow, and on to our hallway carpet dropped this little red envelope with a plain postcard in it, typed out like an invitation.

MR STEVEN BOTTOMLEY
You are cordially invited to an evening of numerous alcoholic beverages followed by a session of <u>possibly</u> orgasmic sexual intercourse (baby oil included if desired at no extra charge). All replies to Andrea .... at your earliest convenience.
Kind regards
Miss Andrea .... 0532 715 ....
(who didn't come the first time but definitely did the second and third, in case you forgot !!)

Jesus, I blushed just reading it. Yeah true, it was a compliment, a big one at that, but it bugged me. If she could send me stuff like that after just one night, what else was there? She might come at me with a glass or start a smear campaign, telling everyone in Leeds that I've got a needledick or that I'm a shit shag.

The line *'Just get a grip on yourself'* suddenly played in my mind and then I laughed. Here was me, bricking it over what a spurned woman might do. What a tosser I was being, some blokes would give their right wrist for the same 'problem'. It dawned on me, *I* was the problem, I wasn't worried about her hurting me, I was worried about *me* hurting me. Forget the Ready Made Family, it was this Randy Male Fuckwit and the reputation I might be making for myself that bothered me. I wanted a steady girlfriend and female company, but I was gagging to sleep with as many women as I could, too. I worked it out: the saying 'The grass is always greener ...' was true, except I was in a desert of lust and virtually any grass would do. But what was a lad to do - wait or search for the chosen one, a princess, or taste the various pleasures and experiences on offer in the meantime?

Gaz was one of the toughest in our year, I was just average. Toughness as a kid is more about having the nerve to fight rather than fighting itself. If I ever needed bailing out of trouble, like when someone wanted me to nick something and not pay me for it, Gaz would sort it out for me, no one wanted to mess with him. We even played alongside each other as centre halves for the football team, anything he didn't win in the air or in a tackle, I'd be positioned a yard or two behind him and sweep up; we were a good partnership. We'd gone to Elland Road that night for the replay against Arsenal, and I told him about me meeting the lads from the Templar, after I'd run from the coppers. He was as keen as I was on meeting up with them, and though it turned out the Saturday match was postponed, we still went. I can't deny it, we were excited like little kids almost, even though we weren't sure if anyone would actually be there. These were some of the Leeds hard cases slated in the daily rags all the time, and you couldn't get more notorious than Leeds hooligans, so they might be hiding.

No worries on that count, the pub was heaving, even early afternoon: blokes standing and sitting around brass topped wrought iron tables, in a fog of cig smoke and conversation. It didn't exactly go deathly quiet like in films but there was a definite drop in the noise as half of them looked at us when we walked in and snaked our way to the bar. After the barmaid served us we stood talking, just whittering really, not knowing what to do or say, hoping no one had taken a dislike to us. Someone had though - I got a tap on the shoulder. It was a fat bloke behind the bar in a white shirt and black beard and he said, so everyone heard, 'Are you old enough to drink here?'

'Yeah ... are you?' cheeky I know but at least I didn't call him Bluto or Jabba, which is what the slob deserved.

'Cheeky little bastard, make it yer last and fuck off home to your mummies.'

'Leave 'em alone Stan, they're alright, they're with us,' a man called from near the door. 'Aren't you lads?'

We looked over, at four or five young blokes around a table, and one grinned and then saluted us with his pint glass.

'Yeah, cheers' I said, and we joined them and a table full of empties and half filled pint glasses.

He introduced, 'I'm Mac, this is Taff, Ziggy and Geordie' and we each exchanged greetings or nods, like boxers before a fight.

I did my bit, 'Steve, and this is Gaz. I met you on the quarry, yeah?' I was pleased, I sounded confident.

'Yeah that's right. You had a bit of a night, didn't you, with that Cockney?' asked Mac.

The lad with the blond flick, Taff, snorted, I wasn't sure if he thought it was funny or if he was being sarc-y.

'I can just about handle them equalizing but he'd gone too far, he was licking Rix's arse nearly. Didn't he Gaz?' a bit of support in case I was making a knob of myself.

'Sure did, mate. Wish I'd done what you did miself'. And he went on to explain how I'd waited for the Arsenal fan to leave the ground to get at him. Gaz never spoke much normally, not because he was thick or anything, just because he was quiet. But now he was telling it like it was his favourite story, and colouring in the details to spice it up. Even I was fascinated, it was that good a tale. '... and then he met you lot on the quarry' he finished.

'Good chance of more of the same at the replay, Steve. You going?' asked Mac.

'Nah, I'm skint Mac, to be honest with yer,' I said.

'Same 'ere' said Gaz.

'Can you make it or not? There's a big crew going down by train on the morning, it'll be a right day.'

Up piped Taff, 'We'll pay for the tickets, you can owe us. Can't they, Mac?'

'Aye, reckon - that is if you *do* wanna go?' said Mac.

'Fucking right we do, eh Steve?' Gaz said.

'You fucking bet!'

'Right then, you're on,' Mac said, and he did a quick drumbeat on the table with his hands. The arrangements were made and now we knew where to meet and what time the train was due.

'And bring some beer, for the journey' chirped Ziggy, whose long, sharp nose and crooked teeth made him look like a rat, and his crew-cut and squat body an ugly one at that.

We stayed in the Templar for hours. Mac and the boys were generous blokes and so me and Gaz hardly bought a beer all day. From what I heard, they earned cash from shoplifting mostly pricey sportswear and electric goods and plenty of it. It put my one boy operation of the past to shame. I got drunker and drunkerer, topping up the previous night's intake and in fact, I got so bolloxed I could hardly string three words together. I decided to leave for a Dewsbury Road bus, the stop just a few yards from the pub door. It was dark when I lurched out in to the well lit night. Gaz stayed, he always could take his beer better than me. The bus driver laughed at me (not too coldly) when I asked for the Broadway stop - vowels and 'ar's drowned in the slavver down my chin.

I hate being out of my tree on buses, other passengers soon work out you're rat-arsed so you try even harder to hide it, and fail miserably. Walking down the aisle and grabbing every seat bar for balance doesn't exactly help conceal the fact, and talking to people you've never met before who aren't very keen on meeting you in the first place just makes things worse. All they see is this pisshead struggling to keep his balance, even when seated, talking complete drivel to anyone unlucky enough to be in the vicinity, finally gently banging his head on the window as he dozes off on the journey.

'Cheers, mate' came out okay as the driver stopped for me on Dewsbury Road, I was a bit more coherent now. My stomach growled and scowled, it'd been hours since I'd eaten and my belly liked to remind me. I ambled up to Larry's chipshop over the road.

'Alright Steve? Been to the Broadway? Pull any Broads?' too many questions.

This was the greeting of the legendary Larry, in his brilliant Alan Ball-like voice that probably most of South Leeds took the piss out of. I wasn't exactly innocent on that count myself in the past, to be honest. I couldn't help but like him, what with the amount of shit he took from punters - especially after the pubs shut - yet he was always cheerful and polite. And clearing up all the chip wrappers and newspapers that lazy bastards hadn't been arsed putting in the dented metal dustbin themselves, he had the patience of a saint; he sure had the chip butties and pickled eggs of one. He needed to sort those shelves supporting the big Ben Shaw's pop bottles out though. Christ, they sagged more than a subs' bench with Ray Hankin and Kenny Burns on it.

His second favourite saying was 'Been to the Blooming Rose? Was it Blooming?' Someone should've discovered this comic talent of his and then buried it for the treasure it was.

Come the morning of the big match, Gaz was waiting outside the Co-op, with some cans of Skol in a plaggy bag. The big cans, not those pointless half size ones with a mouthful of beer in. We caught the number twenty-nine to City Square and met a crowd of twenty or so lads outside the train station bar - the grim City Arms - grimmer still as it was shut.

'Pay us back when you've got it' smiled Mac, as he gave us our tickets for the train and the match.

'Tickets for the game an' all?'

Mac winked, then returned to the others. There was no way of telling that any of us were Leeds fans. Scarves were 'out' and wearing one made you a 'scarfie' or a Christmas tree, and you didn't want to be either. It was 'in' to wear expensive trainers, tracksuit tops made by Fila or Ellesse or Tacchini, or Pringle jerseys of pukey patterns and colours (didn't they see Ronnie Corbett on the box with a different Pringle sweater every week?) Jeans and cords were okay, the cleaner, newer and more expensive, the better. I had a pair of Wranglers on and a thick waffle knit jumper, it was far too cold for a tissue thin tracky top, and my trusted and unpaid for Adidas Bambas. I hated fashion but what do you do? At least the persistent threat of flares coming back never really materialised, you'd never see me in public again if they had, I mean it. In the crowd a couple of fellas wore deerstalker hats, they looked like right twats. Rumour had it they put razor blades under the peaks to use for fighting. This was probably as true as Chelsea Pensioners using their walking sticks to beat opposing supporters. The train wasn't a football 'special', we were on a normal scheduled one, meaning the police were apparently clueless of our existence. With tickets in our pockets, beer chilled for swilling, freedom, no rules and a day trip to London to see our team, we were going to have a right time.

Me and Gaz sat on the train at a table, with Mac and Taff opposite. Over the aisle, Ziggy and Geordie sat with two lads I didn't know. I couldn't get over Ziggy's face. It was hard keeping my eyes off him. When he was born, the midwife fainted I bet, and his mum and dad slapped each other, he was that ugly. Gaz pulled a blinder by producing a pack of cards so for most of the journey our table played Crash. I kept score and was going to adjust them in case I was losing too much dosh but there was no need, we were all about equal, a couple of quid up or down at the most. As the new boys, me and Gaz kept pretty quiet, mostly just enjoying the lads' stories. Tales like at Coventry City when they chased a hotdog seller off, robbed all his cash and handed out free hot dogs and burgers to Leeds fans; and the one about some lads from the Vine pub ransacking a service station in the Midlands and talking in Scouse accents to confuse the staff; and all the battles they'd had and won against other teams, in away pubs or train stations or at motorway services. When the stories were about fighting, Ziggy always had a better one of his own, how he'd done this and done that, kicked the shit out of one rival or knocked ten bells out of another. He had this golden knuckleduster he kept polishing and showing off, posing with it.

Mac whispered to us, 'Take no notice, he wouldn't know how to use it.'

As the train journey progressed southwards, more men joined us at various stations. Those I met seemed alright, I didn't expect them to be the friendliest or trusting of blokes, due to undercover coppers supposed to be infiltrating football gangs. As well as beer, Ziggy had swiped a bottle of Smirnoff to share. I couldn't fault him for his generosity but I was learning he was a nasty piece of work. The way he tried to make himself out harder than the rest and get more attention nearly made me feel sorry for him - nearly. What *really* pissed me off was his hatred for anyone not white or English, or *normal*, 'Crips, Nips and gyps - shoot 'em at birth' and when we were playing cards, every time a spade appeared, out he came with 'black bastards' or 'shoot the niggers' shit, all the time. Worse, I didn't have the guts *not* to smile or laugh, it would have been conspicuous not to. My desire to spit was never stronger than with Ziggy. Eventually, Mac told him to change the record and the nazi fart shut up. I wasn't stupid enough *to* spit at him, because no matter how little I respected him as a person or as a hard-case, I suspected he'd glass me in the face with little fuss if I crossed him. I liked Mac, and Taff seemed okay, he was Mac's right hand man really, and Geordie ... well, I could never really tell, he hardly spoke more than three words at a time and seemed happy enough being there just for the crack. Their nicknames had nothing to do with accents, they were all Leeds born and bred and spoke like the rest of us.

London was an eye opener. I always thought it was supposed to be classy, with better houses, more parks and stuff but from the train, it was no better than up North. What I'd learned in history 'O' level was true, about the railway companies only ever building tracks through slums and the working class areas. Loads of these houses were seedy and decrepit, with broken windows and drainpipes and foreign graffiti all over - what is the point in spraying graffiti if most people haven't a clue or a care about it? You could see inside through the grubby net curtains and blinds. And God knows what the noise must've been like. The thousands and thousands of back to backs in Leeds was bad enough, I didn't expect anything like it down here, not in the capital, where half the world came to visit. We saw Arsenal's stadium Highbury from the train, it wasn't far away, and it made me nervous for a second. We got off. There were no ticket inspectors at King's Cross, and we strolled out on to the big forecourt with black suited tossers in bowler hats, with brollies and briefcases buzzing around, and tourists getting in the way with rucksacks and suitcases and cameras flashing. Only Japs would take photos of a train station, especially a 'picturesque' one like King's Cross. We were easy thirty strong now, and me and Gaz were on a high, we'd really gone up in the world. Members of a team now - a big 'fuck off' team - and no one could stop us and we could do whatever we wanted. And we were just the first wave of crews, there were the National coaches and Wally Trolleys yet, and cars and trainloads: the Cockneys wouldn't know what would hit them. Leeds United might be in the Second Division but *we* were definitely still the top of the League lads.

The plan was, we'd walk to the ground, taking in the sights of North London on the way. These 'sights' were in fact the pubs - Buck House and Big Ben were miles away and didn't matter. This was my first visit to the 'Smoke', all I'd seen before was the usual on TV and films: Marble Arch, Wembley and the Changing of the Guard and stuff, with the Queen and the other Germans pretending to be interested, waving at the commoners and saddo tourists, struggling to stay awake, or sober in certain cases. With the kids' films at the Rex, the opening credits were always Trafalgar Square with pigeons and bright red double decker buses all over, so I imagined all London to be like that but there were no double deckers in sight, only slow moving queues of black cabs and miserable fares and the choke of exhaust fumes which had wiped out any pigeons nearby. From every dark shop doorway blacks and whites looked out for new arrivals and opportunities. The Children's Film Foundation never showed us anything like that. Walking through the streets was great, we were like gangsters, with everyone else avoiding us and looking away. Normally I didn't like it, to see people flinch or shrink, especially your pensioners but this was strangely entertaining.

The pubs we went in were sound, I expected snooty bars, inflated prices and snotty Southerners serving us only when they felt inclined to do so. In fact, they weren't much different to Leeds pubs, except more attractive and neater. One of them was called 'The Dreyer Arms' or something, the others disappeared from my memory, against a wall, and I wasn't even sure of which order we'd visited them in. Beer *was* pricier but not too painful, though the murky liquid out of the electric pumps could hardly be classed as real bitter; the barstaff were always fine, no attitude and not giving a damn about where we were from. We were just about their only customers until late afternoon, so the pubs were ours. Clusters of smaller groups formed, gambling at pool or Space Invaders or the bandits, feeding the jukebox or just sitting around swigging and smoking. The stadium itself is like in the middle of a housing estate, like a Cockney Coronation Street almost, only with taller and better looking houses. I'd never thought but most English football grounds were like this, built in lower class residential areas, just like the railways had been. What were the chances of a big city like Leeds building a stadium in the posh parts such as Alwoodley, or Roundhay? Slimmer than a Kenyan marathon runner, I was sure.

Our last pub was over the road from Highbury. It was about six o'clock and getting busy outside the ground, with coppers conducting traffic and traffic wardens de-conducting it, fast food vendors setting up and early supporters milling around all over the place. I saw a BBC van and TV crew so assumed the game would be on Sportsnight and clips on Look North the night after, with a bit of luck, you could never get enough footie on the telly. In the bar were about forty blokes already, most in red and white scarves or with Arsenal shirts on. Just like The Peacock is the Leeds pub, this looked like it was Arsenal's, with Arsenal mirrors and photographs on the walls and the Gunners cannon motif everywhere. Our number had lessened, to us six plus four or five of the others. We stood out like bacon at a bar mitzvah, though it wasn't a major problem, opposing supporters casually sized each other up and then returned to their business without fuss. I felt quite drunk, not legless but slurring and a bit woozy, and I was aware that besides Gaz, I was easy the youngest in the pub, and the smallest. Ziggy bought a whisky chaser and a pint of lager. He argued with Mac - Mac was telling him to cool down and just enjoy himself - Ziggy was taking no notice. He was steaming drunk, steaming *angry*; he had a look of Jack Nicholson in The Shining, no shit, about to axe his missus to pieces. He downed the whisky in one and then the lager in a quick series of gulps. He held the empty pint glass up as if to examine it, and then threw it at the Arsenal team photo on the wall behind the bar, narrowly missing the barmaid's head, causing her to shriek. The pint glass shattered and left a web of cracks on the photograph.

'For fuck's sake Ziggy!' Mac shouted as he tried to herd us out through the door. He missed me though, and I felt a sharp throttling pain as someone grabbed my jumper collar and yanked me backwards. Angry shouts of 'You facking cants!' followed my mates out of the door but nothing else did - including me. A big fella had me knotted in my sweater and I could hardly do anything save choke, struggle and sag on the spot, looking vainly in the direction of the door. He put a huge fleshy forearm tightly around my throat and sneered into my right ear. Sour bitter-breath poisoned my breathing, 'You're not facking going anywhere, you little wanka.'

I felt like a kitten, humiliated in the jaws of a parent, hanging by the scruff of my neck and awaiting my public punishment. And then the barmaid - the lovely, caring, sweet, *wonderful*, **Mary Poppins** barmaid - shouted, 'Leave 'im alown, it weren't him, he's ownly a kid!'

My Sumo aggressor relaxed his hold, shoving me violently to the door. I smashed into it but I felt nothing and shot out in one smooth motion.

There were clips from around the stadium on TV the next day, mostly of before the game rather than the game itself. I was actually on screen for a few seconds, but it wasn't anything I was proud of. At least I didn't make a complete twat of myself like one lad did, filmed running up behind a fat bloke to kick him up the arse - yeah, real hard stuff - and the dateless bastard missed and nearly did a somersault in the process, landing on his back on the pavement. That was funny but actually being there was no fun, cameras never capture the tension and fear of moments of organized chaos. The noise would normally have been exhilarating but it made me even more scared; a constant engine hum of people talking, shouting and in the distance, chanting. I didn't look frightened but I was, and I was losing it big style. I stood next to the pub doorway, my back to the wall, not wanting to move, not wanting to stay, and clueless where to go. The major worry was I'd lost the rest of them: they'd left me. There were people all around, older people walking and couples with children, and men standing in groups, watching and waiting. Some looked familiar but I couldn't be certain in the dark. To my left dozens of people, normal supporters, were queuing out in to the street, lining up patiently for admittance.

A lad, not much older than me, sprinted by towards a queue of Arsenal supporters. I saw what looked like a Stanley knife in his hand. They didn't see or hear him, they were just waiting - that's all they were doing, waiting, and he stabbed one in the ribs with a punching thrust, and ran away.

There was a savage roar from one man, 'Come on Leeds, get in to 'em!' and groups of men waded into unsuspecting passers by, punching and kicking, even spitting. Some Arsenal lads had their own plan, setting about Leeds fans as well, and pockets of violence erupted all over.

I shrank against the wall, waiting for the chance to flee.

'Did *you* get any action, Steve?' asked Ziggy. It wasn't really a question, the ratfaced bastard knew, I could see it in the shitty, slit-eyed look he gave me, he knew.

'No ... I didn't get chance.'

'Course you didn't, you fucking chicken shit, I saw you run off when it all kicked off.'

'I didn't run off, I lost you lot after the pub so I just went in to the ground, I didn't want to miss the kick off.' This sounded lame even to me.

'*I didn't want to miss the kick off,*' he mimicked.

They were all looking at me, staring, and I heard 'Wanker' and 'Soft bastard' murmured a couple of times.

'Why did you run, Steve?' Mac asked.

Even Gaz was looking at me odd, and when your best mate looks at you with suspicion, it's a lonely feeling.

'I was scared ... alright?' I blurted.

'Scared? **Scared?!** ratface started, 'You fucking little ...'

'You saw the fucking TV cameras, I was scared of getting filmed,' thanks brain, a decent answer, 'I've been bound over to keep the peace for two years ha'en't I, I don't want to be filmed, do I? That's right i'n't it, Gaz?'

And then I snarled, more confident and on a defensive attack, 'I don't want to get fucking nicked and get holed up in fucking Armley jail.' I prayed for the kangaroos to accept my plea.

Gaz nodded. So whether they liked my explanation or not, there it was. I was disgusted - with them and the shithead Ziggy. And with myself. I felt like a guilty brat in a corner, with everyone against me. I struggled out of my seat and shoved between the table and Gaz's knees to the aisle.

'Where're you off to?' Mac asked, calmly. The trial was apparently over. I tried smiling, but a nervous curl of my mouth was all I could manage.

'Just t'bog, mate.'

I didn't need the toilet, just cold water on my burning face and neck. I was sweating cobs and shaking like the proverbial, swaying all over the bleach stinking compartment with the rocking of the train carriage. I stepped out to the end of the carriage and stuck my head out of the slide down door window. The freezing rush of night air refreshed me, taking breath and heat away. Gaz would come looking for me, I was sure. I wasn't going back to them, the shitheads, why should I? It was obvious they hated me, I wasn't part of the team now.

It was Mac who came looking for me.

'Cheer up, Steve, it might never 'appen,' he said brightly, and slapped me on the back like we were old pals.

I knew he knew I was a coward, but unlike ratface he wasn't so *tough* as to single me out for a public 'execution'. He hadn't been far wrong with that old saying that it *might* never happen; only I went further: this situation would *definitely* **never** happen for me. Football hooliganism wasn't my game one hundred per cent and I'd been completely full of shit. What the fuck had I been thinking about before? What an arsehole, I was never tough as a kid and I wasn't suddenly going to change as I grew older, no matter how strong the appeal.

After the Arsenal game at Highbury, where in the face of fighting I'd shat myself, I hardly saw Gaz again. I wasn't the only one. He replaced us - his regular Friday and Saturday night drinking pals - with a new, madder, more exciting crew.

It pissed me off in a big way: not only had I made an arse of myself, I'd lost my best mate to Mac and that lot because of it. Fortunately, there were others to keep my social calendar alive, mainly Gaz's elder brother Mike and his mates who'd let us jump on board their beer bandwagon when we'd first started boozing. These lads spoke *with* each other and laughed more together and their aim was to steer towards women and away from any scrapping.

This exile from the football mob didn't stop my enjoyment hearing about their exploits or scare me off supporting Leeds. Nothing could do that; I've never understood how anyone stopped supporting a team; it's like turning your back on a close relation because they're ill or something. I didn't need to be a part of the 'trouble' to be proud of it, even if that **is** a twisted and chicken point of view. I don't mean the kicking shit out of innocent fans or stabbing people or trashing a stadium - all of that is bollocks, total bollocks - I mean the unofficial English civil wars cropping up all over the place, on the terraces and outside the soccer grounds. It was often more exciting to watch the running battles than what we had to endure on the pitch, certainly with Leeds United, no getting away from it. We Leeds fans didn't have a lot to shout about in a football sense but at least off the park we knew we had a white-hot team with us. This opinion made me a hypocritical twat I know but I felt no guilt, it could have been me with only a little tweak of reality: I could have been worse even, running with the pack but at the back like a cowardly mutt, egging them on from the background, waiting for the chance to 'prey' on someone once they were already beaten.

The most worrying thing for us normal, decent supporters was that in her wisdom, the cunt at Number 10 and her slime of sycophants had heaped all of the blame on to the people who ran football, as if nothing else similar was happening in Britain. The Football League in turn had scant choice but to punish the relevant clubs by fining or banning them and even threatening them with closure (expulsion from the English League), which is what Leeds were definitely heading towards. We'd never been popular with the League as it was, since the early seventies when *evil* Leeds supporters had taken exception to a certain referee named Tinkler for allowing West Brom a goal which was more offside than the glam flares and platform shoes of the day. A few supporters invaded the pitch as his decision effectively robbed us of the Championship. Ever since then, Leeds fans were high in the list of UK public enemies, along with Man U, Chelsea, Spurs, Millwall and so on. During our European campaigns it wouldn't have surprised me to see the gutter papers showing pictures of the Coliseum or other famous continental ruins with the caption 'ENGLISH FANS TO BLAME - AGAIN!' The only reason the 'sweaty socks', sorry 'Jocks', sorry *Scots* never got slagged off is because they're always too pissed up to do *anything* other than sing, puke and start drinking again.

It was obvious to me that the night's events at Arsenal weren't only the end of me and Gaz as best buddies: it was the beginning of an addiction for him, too. He'd told his brother that he'd never experienced anything to compare with the thrill of fighting in a team and no friendship is stronger than one built in battle (he really said that), like an unbreakable bond: it was the most exciting buzz he'd ever come across. He'd smashed one Arsenal fella so hard in the face that the gadger's nose had broken *and* he'd managed to fight off a 'Pig' and his dog, smacking the copper in the face and christening his size tens in the ribs of the now yelping Alsatian. Gaz hadn't suddenly changed into a maniac, he proved this by slagging off the wanker who'd knifed the Arsenal fella queuing to get in for the game, and word had it he'd slated Ziggy for his antics before and after the match as well. I took a bit of comfort from this as I think he was referring to what the ugly little fucker had put me through on the train home. I would have preferred to hear that Gaz had kicked ratface's teeth in.

Gaz now had a near celebrity status in certain quarters of Leeds, renowned as one of LUFC's top boys, scared of nothing and happy to 'get stuck in'. He gloried in the rewards that came with his new reputation, like the expensive sports gear given or sold to him 'off the back of a lorry', the easy shags with birds from Nellie's and Stallone's, and drinks and poppers regularly bought for him. Well, this is what I heard anyhow, not that I had any reason to doubt it, I was jealous in fact. We'd had some great laughs knocking around with Mike and his mates but now Gaz had his new allies and was more interested in their adventures. Deep down, I knew he'd lost respect for me and I can't say I really blamed him for it - even if it was through me he'd met Mac and co. A friendship without respect is not a friendship worth carrying on with.

The authorities never seemed to realise that the more they tried to prevent hooliganism, the more fun it was for those guilty of it. It was all a huge, nationally networked game, gangs holding their own much more thrilling 'matches' away from the football pitch, and the police weren't invited. If the law wanted to attend, they'd have to gatecrash and fight both sides, which they usually did, wading in with their truncheons and helmets. It was fair enough; hooligans were fair game. Their problem was they ran greater risk of creating their own notoriety and behaving worse than their targets, similar to how the London Met had treated the pickets during the Miners' Strike and other industrial actions in the eighties. They had more to lose *and* there was a strong chance they'd receive a good kicking in the process. Even if arrests were made, it was hardly ever a closed book. We heard in courts across the country:

'My client received cuts and bruising to the forehead from the constable's helmet as it was deliberately brought crashing down on my client's head.'

or

'My client was merely an innocent bystander, unfortunate to be in the wrong place at the wrong time, clearly set upon by opposing football supporters and then wrongfully arrested for his troubles.'

Even more ridiculous was when undercover officers were planted to infiltrate the hooligan factions, which happened in Leeds and probably a host of other cities. What a laugh, did they really think it would work, that their 'evidence' would stand up in court? Until you've seen all the planning and organization that went in to setting up a 'meet' with opposing crews, you'd never believe how efficient this brand of anarchy could be. It was more like the gangs had infiltrated the police than the other way around, usually being one step ahead and aware of the force's plans for each game before the plod did, and learning the travel arrangements of away fans and the road and rail timetables, even down to petrol and service station stops on the motorways. The powers that be would never prevent it, especially with a government blaming every one but themselves for society's troubles, the wars on the terraces being just one of many. There were many like Gaz who planned to enjoy this brand of footballing adventure for as long as they were able to.

A Job's Worth ...

I'm not clever enough - or sufficiently arsed - to comment but I do know that in the eighties, if you were on the dole and skint, you didn't get much understanding from the media or government or our 'loadsamoney' society. No surprise about the first two there, I was embarrassed by what most of the papers printed, backing the government in every argument, every scandal, and glorying in the slaughter of every opponent. It was when grabbing everything you could get your grubby paws on was regarded as a virtue and **fuck you** if you weren't getting your share.

It was so easy to sneer and scoff at unemployed people as one big group of workshy skiving scroungers; it was almost encouraged in fact. Even OAPs did it, with their tartan shopping trolleys trundling behind them, looking down their noses as you cashed your Giro at the local post office. If they knew the shit a lot of us went through - depression, insomnia, lethargy, boredom - they might have thought differently. Probably not though, you see, if the government repeats something enough times they eventually believe their own lies and statistics themselves, with most of the population nodding in agreement like congregations of those fucking toy dogs. So *really,* there were hundreds of thousands of quality jobs available, 'they' ie. **me**, simply weren't looking hard enough for them, that was all. I was on the dole for nearly a year after leaving school. And whose fault was it? Well, mostly mine actually, I can't deny it. I'd tossed it off at school, I was more bothered about having a laugh and truanting for X films at the Odeon than revising for my O levels.

So I'd loused up my education, I could still get a job easy. Except I wouldn't apply for any job, I wasn't going to do deadend work or a Youth Opportunity Programme *stroke* Youth Training Scheme (same shit, different banner). Okay, I couldn't prove it with many certificates but I was a bright enough lad and I deserved a chance, or so I believed. I know what that probably looks like but in my defence, you should have seen what jobs *were* available. One of the first to leave at sixteen was a lad called Duffield and he got a job fixing the heads on

Action Man figures. Dead proud he was an' all, getting sixty quid a week for it. I knew him well enough to think he was better than that. I knew myself well enough to know *I* definitely bloody was.

My mum put down a few rules whilst I was on the dole, seeing as I was getting about twenty quid a week without paying board. I didn't like it at the time but she was right to, and it helped me keep quite disciplined. When you've nothing to get out of bed for, it's amazing how tired you always feel. I got up at nine nearly every day, as much a pain in the arse as it was. Listening to my records 'til two/three o'clock in the morning didn't help but I couldn't sleep unless I went to bed late. If telly hadn't have closed down at midnight, that might have helped. A good piece of advice for anyone pissed off: don't play too many Joy Division, Cure, PiL or even Doors records, they can mess your head up, I swear. The only reason you'd want to get out of bed would be to throw yourself out the bedroom window.

While my mum went to work I did most of the shopping and washing up. I even went to meet our kid from school every now and then and cooked all our teas. She taught me how to use the washer/dryer and how to iron, which she especially enjoyed. Not that I actually did any. And in between all of this, I applied for decent jobs, and wrote to companies I thought I'd like to work for. Leeds/Bradford Airport was one of them. The bastards never even replied. They weren't the only ones either, I forget the others which is a pity because one day I'd have loved to get my own back on them. It's a fucking low punch, not replying to someone who wants to work for you; and worse still are the wankers who advertise vacancies and then don't reply to your job application - what's all that about?

The worst time of all was when I applied to be a postman. I made it on to a final shortlist of six, out of 1200 (*twelve hundred*) applicants. I had my second interview at Royal Mail's HQ on Wellington Street and I reckoned it had gone well. After two weeks I'd not heard anything so I rang them to ask if they'd decided yet - they hadn't. Another week went by and I rang again - they *had* decided and told me I'd hear from them shortly. After another sodding week I rang again and they said they'd get back to me. After a total of four weeks and one day I rang again. They then asked me if I'd received the letter in the post sent a few weeks before, saying I'd been unsuccessful. Cry? I nearly laughed.

It wasn't all bad news, I had one interview after the Royal Mail fiasco where if it had been someone else I would have pissed my pants laughing. It was as a clerical officer for a Leeds mail order company. Think of going for a job you really want, one you're sure you'd be good at and one you've been building up to the interview of for days before. In fact, you want it so much you need to have three craps before leaving home on the morning. You get there and are eventually called in for the one to one interview with the office manager Eric Kay - a late forties chap in a very plush grey suit and royal silk tie - you wipe your hand on your kegs when he's not looking to ensure you don't give a sweaty cod handshake. In the room there are two low soft chairs with a little coffee table between. You wait for him to say 'Please, sit down' and when he does you both bend to sit and you headbutt him on the forehead with such a clout Yosser Hughes would have cheered. Was I embarrassed - it isn't a question - yeah, just a bit, so I blurted 'That's in case you don't take me on!' to try and make light of the uncommon assault. The interview was irrelevant after that and I was praying for it all to be over with quickly - similar to my morning in the clap clinic - so I could go home and die. I was down for a few days after, I thought I'd screwed up good and proper this time, a big chance wasted. Notice I don't say depressed, because that's a completely different kettle of shit. I learned to take the usual blows on the chin though this was harder because it was self-inflicted. Anyway, no matter, because when I'm wrong, I'm really wrong and this time, I was wrong. God was I: Eric Kay wrote to me to offer me the job. I rang him up straight away to thank him and probably embarrassed myself again. It must have been about my fifteenth job interview in all so you can guess the degree of my chuffed-ness. My mum was delighted as well and I even let her kiss me to celebrate (just the once); now I could look the lads in the eye and be able to buy *them* a drink for a change.

It's always better over the garden fence so they say, except when you live in a high rise I suppose, and I soon realised working for a living was a ball acher of relative proportions (I did like the feeling of having earned a good night's kip, though). I don't know about the state running the media and stuff, I felt like I was being brainwashed by some unknown ruler, in 'How to Deal With Irate Customers' and 'Respect Your Fellow Employees' sort of crap. 'Hang Up on Them' and 'Only Be Nice to People Who Are Nice to You' were two of my favourite attitudes, unofficially mind. In reality, I tried to get on with everyone and get on with the job which in itself I found interesting. I was good at it an' all and I'd learned enough on the dole to know which side my bread had dripping on. My main task was chasing the *Late Cash* of mail order 'agents' who were behind on their and their customers' payments for Christmas hampers which they paid for in instalments. I had to warn them there'd be no hamper deliveries and that they'd be blacklisted if we didn't get the cash. Eventually, if they were still owing, I'd threaten them with legal action which actually meant our passing the accounts on to debt collection companies who would obtain the payments by whatever means. Some of these cases ended up with agents getting a beating from the collectors and the bailiffs being called in. Most of these agents were on the dole.

You know, a lad can make a mistake. Okay, in my case I'd have to multiply the plea a few times but I was never that wayward, I just boarded the wrong mind train at times and I did usually learn from my mistakes. So it always surprised me for people to think I might have been involved in any scrapes or trouble. Early in my job it dawned on me that most people there weren't interested in the slightest about the beautiful game, certainly not the women in my department, anyhow. All they appeared keen on was the gossip in the smoke room and the canteen breaks; oh, and their jobs, mustn't forget that. This isn't really me being snotty about them – these ladies were mainly ace to work with and dead nice to me – but a criticism aimed at the whole customer services world and attitude as it's 'developed' over the years. If you're treated like a simple cog in a machine you're going to take on a less caring attitude to the people who pay your wages (the customer, in other words) and so they all become just another set of whingers, whether they ring in or write.

Fortunately in those days, we had more of a 'free-range' office: call centre battery farms and commodes at the desks came later. Our office dealt with all the agents' accounts, hamper orders and correspondence (by phone or by letter) and it was a well run, efficient and busy operation. Our customers – besides ourselves naturally, we're all customers, remember - were the general public, thousands who'd become agents for us, collecting money on a weekly basis from their clients (neighbours, friends, *cellmates* and so on) and who sent us the dosh every month with the relevant accounts sheets. I found it all fairly enjoyable to be honest, which came as a surprise even to me: it meant using my brain. What I liked most was the 'bad debt' side, where agents had collected money from people and either blatantly not sent it in to us or tried ripping those people off by not filling in the clients' account sheets correctly and asking for more cash. These tossers never got away with it – not as far as I was involved any rate – and after a few months in the job nothing was more fun for me than putting together threatening letters to the agents or even better, the chance to have a go at them over the phone. And if that didn't work, I'd pass the thieving toe-rags' accounts on to the real bruisers, the pucker debt collectors.

The lasses in our office treated me really well - the older ones would look after me like I was a favourite nephew or son and the younger ones would have a laugh with me as well as turn me on, not that I ever let them know. There was only one other fella in the department and that was Eric who had his own little private office in the corner. Everyone knew I was a Leeds fan but when they read the stuff in the daily rags about supporters wreaking havoc all the time, I got tired of being asked if I'd been involved. Couldn't they take it in that not everyone who followed Leeds around the country wanted to fight? Stupid question, and so now instead of once been guilty of fighting, I had a fight to be seen as innocent. Strange but in the end, I knew that if work colleagues really did think I was in to scrapping, I wouldn't have very long left in the job. At least I had black mates at work - well one, Ev from the post room - so they could see I wasn't a *nazi* hooligan, that would have been too much.

Having to be associated with racism was shite. It was bad enough being suspected as a hooligan but that was something I really couldn't complain about seeing as if I'd been as hard as I'd liked, I'd have still been best mates with Gaz and causing bother all over the country with that crew. At least with the trouble on the terraces, most clubs in England had the same problem, but with the racism, Leeds seemed to suffer more than most, even though they were in a small minority. The papers and politicians loved to point foul smelling fingers of accusation at Leeds United and us supporters as if it wasn't happening anywhere else. They *overlooked* that being a well supported team in one of the highest populated cities meant that there were bound to be elements of every belief and political view in the crowds and when things are going badly in a country, it doesn't take much for society's sickoes and extremist knobheads to appear with their hatred and violence. This didn't just happen on the terraces, it happened everywhere in England. It wasn't too different to what happened in Germany in the thirties - I'd read enough about Hitler and co to learn that much - it was to their shame our educated politicians and journalists couldn't or wouldn't see it. What better place for fascists or nazis, or whatever these wankstains called themselves, to be heard and spread their poison than on the terraces? In a crowd they'd get away with it, starting gorilla grunts or 'sieg Heils' or lobbing bananas on to the pitch whenever a black player was appearing, and rely on some sad twat to join in, and the next, and the next…. Leeds United wasn't as badly afflicted as Chelsea and Millwall and West Ham and a few others, but we still had enough trash to deal with, that was for sure. If you were black and you actually went to the matches, all I can say is that you were brave in a big way. But what did I know about it, about how it really must feel to be singled out in a crowd or to be persecuted that way? Okay, I knew it wasn't right - none of it was right, it's never been right and it never will be right - so maybe I deserve a tiny bit of credit but I was too much of a coward to do anything about it, to try to stop it. Yes, I walked by silently scowling at the lowlife handing out their filth publications on Lowfields Road and 'Spit' Bottomley was on target a couple of times - on their backs so they could never see who'd done it - but I wasn't brave enough to make a real stand against them.

The 31st of October 1984 was a memorable day for the people of the city of Leeds, and it had nothing to do with Hallowe'en, this was horrific enough on its own. Two Leeds policemen, Sergeant John Speed and PC John Thorpe had been questioning two suspicious looking men near the Leeds Parish Church around midday. One of the men pulled a gun and shot Sergeant Speed dead and seriously injured PC Thorpe. Another bobby who was in the vicinity, PC Raj, was shot at but not hit. That same night, Leeds were at home to Watford in the League Cup and on paper it was quite a big game for us. They'd never played each other before, Watford had always been this little lower division lot, and Leeds had always been the big, famous team in all white from the North. Now, Leeds were languishing in Division Two whilst Watford were in the First. This was a chance for Leeds to prove the positions were the wrong way around: I mean, Watford in the First Division, us below? To be fair to Watford, they'd made a decent reputation for themselves as an entertaining, attacking team and had a few class players, like John

Barnes and Nigel Callaghan, for instance. Two of their best players were black and played for England - Barnes on the left wing and Luther Blissett at centre forward - which upset plenty of the Anglo Saxon cavemen down at Wembley Stadium. I was worried, not just because I thought Watford would hammer us but because of their black players: I thought their presence would bring out the swastika brigade in force (it was Hallowe'en after all) and that they'd really drop the club in it (as in getting closed down). I didn't want to even think about what life would be without football.

Before the game, official police requests were played over the Elland Road sound system for people to come forward if they had any information on Sergeant Speed's murder. I knew nothing; I wished I did. Rumours that it was terrorist linked turned out to be untrue. I was really surprised at how much the shootings had affected the crowd - not in the attendance, it was quite big - but that it was eerily quiet with hardly a song or chant. I can't deny it, the more I thought about Sergeant Speed's murder, the more upset I became with the memories of my dad dying flooding my head.

Watford wiped the floor with Leeds, beating us four nil. They'd torn us apart with Barnes controlling the game, Blissett winning everything up front and Callaghan slicing the defence apart at his leisure. And they had this little black lad called Sterling in attack who was like lightning. He scored one and helped set up a couple of others. When he scored, I half expected some twat to shout 'jungle bunny' or something not as clever but there was hardly any reaction. I was relieved.

Obviously, I was pissed off we'd lost - how many times must you be hurt by your team? - but that pain paled compared to what everyone had felt for Sergeant Speed and his family. Strange but I had a strong feeling of pride: in the police who'd lost one of their own, and in the public who shared the grief and shock, and in the Leeds United crowd who had always roared on the team *whatever*, but tonight a voice of quiet showed more respect and support for a completely different team.

Great quotes from the Beautiful Game :

'The keeper's a clown' - Brian Clough preaching about Poland's goalie, Tomaszewski in 1973.

'Mmm, that bracelet's nice' - Bobby Moore, in Columbia before the Mexico World Cup in 1970.

'I'm not getting in the way of that bastard' - any defender near a Peter Lorimer shot.

And maybe the most famous 'Some people think football is a matter of life and death......it is much more serious than that' - Bill Shankly.

Shankly - 'Shanks' - was always popular with Leeds supporters over the years, or at least they respected him. He and Don Revie were the best managers around and good, friendly opponents (Matt Busby was okay an' all but that pains me to say it). Leeds-Liverpool games had always been special and there was usually a good natured and healthy rivalry between opposing supporters. In fact, when Leeds had needed a draw at Anfield to win the League in 1969 - and got it - the Liverpool fans on their Kop had chanted 'Champions' to the Leeds team - *that's* real sport for you. It was the same Liverpool crowd that took the piss out of Gary Sprake when he threw the ball in to his net once by singing 'Careless Hands' to him. Scousers really could be funny at times.

After I stopped going to Leeds away games with Gaz and his mates I joined the Fullerton Park branch of the Supporters Club with Paul, a mate from work who was now one of my regular drinking partners. We'd get rat-arsed on the Friday night and then roll up for the coach on Elland Road the next morning, still drunk. The Fullerton had a committee to arrange all the transport and match tickets and Player of the Year votes and stuff, but for us it had always been run unofficially by Robert Banks and his beard. The best thing about the Fullerton bunch was that they viewed having a few jars before every game as essential, nearly as important as the match itself, and Banksy was definitely the leader of that party. They were a friendly lot - mainly older than me and Paul - and treated us well. I think they admired us for the wrecked states we turned up in, to be honest. Booze wasn't allowed on the coach - except what was in your bloodstream of course - so we relied on Banksy to sniff out good boozers around England in preparation for Leeds's away games nearby. On this particular Saturday it was the last day of the season and Leeds had a remote chance of reaching the Division Two promotion play offs if we beat Birmingham City away; City themselves were already promoted but had to win to go up as the champions of the division. Unfortunately, all the pubs in and around Birmingham were shut, the whole of the West Midlands seemingly expecting crowd trouble before the game. It was understandable, they were right. The Fullerton was never in to that sort of stuff, visiting pubs on their travels had always been fun enough. I had the best of both worlds, enjoying the beers as well as later enjoying hearing about the various battles and riots the gangs had been involved with. Banksy had managed without fail to get us in to nice village or country pubs with every away game I'd been to with the Fullerton, until this time. Eventually, our driver found a Safeway on the outskirts of Birmingham, though we had to sit in the car park to drink our beer and spirits purchases. At least someone produced a football and we were able to have a decent kickabout though it wasn't the same standard of pre-match entertainment we'd become accustomed to.

Probably only the police knew why they made us wait outside the steel gates of City's St Andrew's ground rather than let us in to the stadium. And what a shit tip it was outside, no buildings just ugly khaki wasteground. There were scores of Leeds fans already waiting and not surprisingly, the nearer it got to three o'clock kick off the more pissed off we became. It wasn't long before rocks and half bricks were raining down on the policemen positioned between the gate and us. What those tossers doing the throwing hadn't realised was that their missiles were closer to hitting their fellow supporters rather than the coppers, and we didn't have frigging helmets on. The longer we had to wait and the shorter the odds of me getting lamped by stray friendly fire, the more I was tempted to launch a missile of my own. 'Spit' Bottomley was kept in check and Paul decided to ask them why there was a delay. He'd been in the police himself a few years before so he knew how to talk to the uniforms. He was told it was 'Orders from above'. Ah right, so long as we knew - who exactly then, was it Jesus? The dicks. The crowd was increasing rapidly and we were being pushed more and more right in to the coppers' faces. All *they* did was push us back, which was even more a pain in the neck. Finally we were allowed in about half an hour before kick off but the mood wasn't what you'd call pretty: when a West Midlands bobby had a thought, it spent a long and lonely journey crossing his mind, we'd witnessed it.

In the stadium we had a small corner section. On the right was another covered stand - the 'away' seats - and on our left a gap with a fence at each side separating City from Leeds a few yards across. Away supporters having shelter was something of a luxury but we weren't really that impressed: strangely for England, specially in summertime, it was hot and sunny. We chose to stand at the top of the terracing, the highest step just a few feet below the roof. It'd become a ball ache standing near the front at away games, watching the match whilst arseholes tried to rip the fences down; get on the pitch and disrupt the game. And if that wasn't enough, coins and ball bearings thrown at the culprits by objectors to the chaos regularly smacked you nicely on the back of the head. It was fair enough Kevin Keegan getting that treatment maybe but not us. Despite how we'd been wound up already, the crowd was surprisingly quiet; for Leeds to qualify for the play offs would have needed a miracle, and we never got those. Don Revie had actually believed the club had been cursed by an old gypsy woman years before and he might well have been right. There was no doubt that the only luck Leeds United ever had was bad luck.

By the time the blue and whites of City and the yellows of Leeds had lined up on the pitch to start the match, the police had closed the gates and locked dozens of Leeds fans out of the ground. This meant that even though our section was packed overall, there were still gaps around us near the back of the terracing so I decided I'd watch the game in comfort, sitting on a barrier. I stood in front of my chosen 'throne' and reached back with both hands so as to haul myself up. I shot up, aiming to land my backside safely on to the bar. Something then entered my head that this hadn't been a very good idea - *something* being the edge of an overhanging steel girder of the roof. I remember hurtling toward the ground - like when a newsman falls or drops his TV camera and your vision is all over the place - and I woke up on my back on the concrete. I'd been unconscious for a few seconds apparently, and focussed to see Paul and a couple of other chaps looking down at me.

Jesus, there was pain.

'Shit the bed Steve, you alright?' Paul asked. I quickly ascertained he'd retained that skill from the force of asking sensible questions. I couldn't answer.

One of the other men ordered me to stay still, I wasn't exactly desperate to do a sequence of starjumps, that was for sure.

FUCK FUCK FUCK, it hurt, with a stinging and skull-cracking headache like the worst hangover ever, and extended. I fingered my scalp, immediately regretting it as wetness warmed my fingertips.

'Oh bollocking hell,' said Paul, as lines of crimson trickled down my forehead and increased to thicker, darker streams. Blood began to seep in to my eyes and pour off the end of my nose and chin. Obviously, I couldn't say what it all looked like but it *felt* like I had a gushing bloody oil strike in the middle of my cranium. The other chap donated his scarf and Paul padded it to my head, telling me to hold it there to stem the flow of blood. He then helped me get to my feet and guided me out to a ginnel where two policemen were standing, observing us approach through the bars of an iron gate. There were lots of angry voices from outside the ground and I could tell the gate we'd used earlier was getting a real pummelling, with what I never found out.

'My laddo here's had an accident and banged his head. Can you get him some attention, please gents?' Paul asked.

What **was** it with Midlands coppers and me? Or did they hate all football fans, or just Northerners? Their reaction - or lack of it, to be more accurate - was a verbal shrug of the shoulders and a 'What do you want *us* to do about it?' sort of thing. For all those two helmets knew - and me as a matter of **non-fact** - I could have been dripping there with a fractured skull or even damage to my grey matter. I'd permanently ruined the bloke's scarf, *that* was a fact.

Paul kept his cool, explaining to Tweedle Dumb and Tweedle Dim what had happened; and all without the aid of diagrams, too. One Tweedle then radioed through to someone while the other unchained the gate and let me through. Paul was ordered to return to the match.

'You been a naughty boy then, sonny Jim?' one asked me while we waited. Shouldn't there have been three *'ello*'s at the start of that question?

'No mate, I was throwing bricks at you lot and I've never been that good a shot.'

They didn't laugh. I was a prick to think they would have. 'No really, I jumped up to sit on a barrier and cracked my head on a girder.'

'Course you did.'

I wasn't going to argue, I'd have only got nicked or smacked - or both - I was pretty sure of it. The St John Ambulance lady who came to escort me was ace, though nervous for some reason. Maybe she was concerned about Birmingham's notoriously risky offside tactics. She led me back in to the stand and down through the fenced off gap between the rival sets of fans to the edge of the pitch behind the goal. The game was in full flow and she grabbed my arm in case I attempted a one man pitch invasion. *Do me a favour, lady,* what do you think I am?

As we walked in front of the Leeds fans I heard a large round of applause and thought one of our players had done something good, but when I looked on the pitch there was nothing really going on. I looked up to the thousands of Leeds fans and realised clusters of thirty or forty were clapping me. ***Jesus,*** *do me another favour!* You could have seen me blushing with embarrassment if it hadn't have been for the pints of life force plastering my head. The horrible vision of Ziggy appeared in my mind, grinning like a gargoyle and I wondered if he was one of those clapping me. To more personal shame I suddenly hoped he had and I got this surge of pride that made me want to throw up next to the pitch. Now *that* would have been an achievement. I put this schizo reaction down to having very nearly split my head in half. As we passed the Leeds dugout at the side of the pitch, I looked down at the substitutes' bench to see our manager, Eddie Gray, fixed on the game and the sub Andy Ritchie looking up at me, horrified. I was touched, he looked really worried. I wanted to say, 'It's not what it looks like, Andy, honest mate' but I didn't get the chance as the St John woman was walking too quickly, nearly dragging me away. I grinned sheepishly and shook my head at him. This made me even dizzier. She guided me down a tunnel and in to a busy room, and closed the door after her.

Men (other casualties) were seated around the room and St John uniforms were attending to them. I was placed in a chair next to a City fan a few years older than me. Suddenly the door banged open as a huge black bloke in a blue Adidas tracksuit kicked it. He was obviously one of City's 'Zulu Warrior' we'd heard about. He demanded medical attention and I thought he must be badly hurt or something. I wouldn't have argued with him whatever his problem, I was clear enough in my mind to decide that much. The lady rushed over to see to him and then firmly but politely asked him to await his turn outside and she closed the door after him and locked it. It turned out he'd been fighting some Leeds lads and had had a Stanley knife swung at him, ripping his tracksuit top but only scratching his arm: 'Zulu Worrier' more like.

The man next to me had a swollen cheek and bloodied nose. He looked at me and noticed the blood sodden Leeds scarf on my head. It didn't deter him from offering his hand to me and so we shook. He told me he'd been walking to the match when four or five Leeds fans came running in the opposite direction, taking a pop at anyone in front of them. This guy had been set on by three of them, he thought. The poor sod, this wasn't in the rules, he wasn't a willing participant. We were interrupted by a St John chap who decided I was an urgent case - not just because of the severity of my injury but due to the fact I was the only Leeds supporter in there.

He was a pensioner but his age didn't detract from his handiwork with cotton wool and stinging antiseptic. He had to really scrub at my nose to get rid of the dried blood and that hurt enough on its own. Really, he explained, I should have been taken to hospital for stitches as they didn't have the necessary facilities in the stadium. I didn't fancy going to a 'foreign' hospital so they agreed to clean up the cut and mend my damaged nut the best they could with 'plastic skin'. Whilst this had been going on the Brummie bloke next to me had carried on talking about how he'd been to Leeds and thought it a lovely city. I didn't tell him how I thought what I'd seen of Birmingham was a shithole but I did apologise for him being beaten up. As the lady helped me out of my seat, me and the Brum bloke shook hands again, like good old mates.

As I walked away, he said - and I'll never forget it - 'I wish all Leeds fans were like you.' It wasn't long ago I could have been one of those punching him, but I didn't dwell on that.

Back on the terraces with Paul at half time, it became obvious plenty of people weren't bothered about the football, they had their own plans. Leeds lads - and most of them were lads, younger than me - about forty of them, had begun their fence demolishing, causing a long cordon of policemen to form in front of them to stop them getting on the pitch or to drag those out who'd ventured too far and arrest them. Naturally, for want of a better word, the continuous dismantlement was riling the City fans. The police - still lined up in front and facing us - were clueless as to what was now happening elsewhere: City supporters from all parts of the stadium were running on to the pitch and approaching them. It was comical to begin with - a slow motion pantomime with villains creeping up on their unwitting victims - but we then realised that it was likely to get much more serious. We started to shout warnings of 'Watch out, you daft bastards!' and the like but they obviously couldn't hear.

Fortunately, the DJ was alert to it all and in true panto fashion, began to cry, 'Behind you, behind you!' to the police, and 'Police officers on the pitch, *look behind you!*' as the hordes of fans got nearer. He deserved a medal did that DJ. The police officers on the pitch finally sussed out that *they* were the said police officers on the pitch and chased the mob off, leaving the Leeds fans to their metalwork again. The referee wouldn't start the second half of the game until the anarchy had settled and the Leeds mob wouldn't stop ripping down the fencing and trying to get on the pitch, despite the fact that most of us were against them. I noticed that most of the men pulling the fencing down had no intention whatsoever of going on to the pitch, as if they were 'allowing' others to do it first. Eventually, Eddie Gray took it upon himself to help to sort it all out and came and stood on the corner of the pitch in front of us, and pleaded for all the trouble to stop. It seemed to work as the crowd went quiet and those at the front climbed down. Eddie had been one of the most popular Leeds players ever, a genuine and good man with a talent comparable to Best and better than the rest, but then darting flashes appeared over the crowd as a dozen or so coins flew towards him. He seriously wasn't the only one shocked by that. He shook his head in despair and though I wasn't close enough to see, I just knew he was in tears. He turned around with a gesture of bitter defeat and hopelessness, and walked away. The scum who threw those coins weren't fit to be called Leeds fans; it was fucking appalling what they did. If ever there was a time when I considered losing my allegiance, it was then.

The match eventually did restart and City won one nil. When we got back to the coach, we were the last to arrive.

Banksy said, 'Thank God you're back, a Leeds lad's been killed!'

At first we didn't have a clue what he was talking about. They'd heard it on the radio that a wall had collapsed, crushing a teenager and killing him. As we were travelling back to Leeds, even worse news followed, this time from near home, *very* near home, in Bradford. There'd been a fire in the main stand of the football ground Valley Parade. I'd sat in the very same stand a couple of years before and I remembered how virtually all of it had been made of wood, even the floor. To begin with, the reports mentioned just the possibility of a couple of casualties but I was less hopeful. I wasn't proud to do it but I predicted the news would get worse.

And it did. The next reports were of a possible few deaths. The final reports confirmed that the possible had turned to a definite, and the few had grown to fifty-six. **May 11th, 1985**.

After the toil of pushing of pen one day, I was sardined on the bus home, passing the New Canning Club at the bottom of Dewsbury Road. Looking over to the South Leeds Sports Centre pitches where some of Beeston's finest regularly played, I saw what I thought was a small monument in the foreground: a black plaque set on a grey base and background. I guessed it was about three feet square in all, the base or plinth looked to be marble, and on it the black plaque. I was interested; no, I was actually quite excited and I wondered why it was there, whose memory it could be for and so on. I'd always thought of the Leeds authorities as shoddy for their lack of commemorating favourite sons and daughters and heroes and heroines of the city but now possibly they'd pulled their fingers out at last. Perhaps that was harsh but it's how I felt. Fair enough, we had schools named after Hugh Gaitskell and Matthew Murray (who was Abbey Grange, by the way?) but it's not exactly 'in your face' local pride. On a slightly different tack, I always thought it very poor that the refrigerated gas chambers on Soldiers' Field (in reality, changing rooms) were still in use, regardless of the fact that the bastard Yorkshire Ripper had murdered one of his victims behind one block. Not a word was said or anything, *so what* if she was a prostitute? Yes, it's possibly the lowest, seediest career other than pimping but she was still a human being, and we all sell ourselves one way or another.

I'd long thought Leeds had been barren of talent or that no one cared about famous 'Loiners', as if it might be too embarrassing to draw attention to ourselves. We should follow Liverpool's example: if such a city can sing the praises of Cilla Black and Jimmy Tarbuck and other 'luminaries' then there's hope for us all. The city of Leeds *wasn't* proud or loud enough - like England in general - patting gallant losers heartily on the back whilst stabbing winners in theirs at the same time. And it was like we were banned from mentioning the World Wars, as if to do so would cause upset or be offensive. WHO TO? You can fuck those sentiments **right** off for me, I tell you, I'd be proud to wear a poppy all the year round and so would many more, to show that we *do* respect and care about those millions (MILLIONS) sacrificed in the fight against the worst enemy in history. Honouring your War Dead and War Heroes doesn't make you a war monger, that's the (ir)responsibility of the politicians. So what was this monument about?

In my twelfth and thirteenth years, hardly a day went by without my hearing The Beatles and I was often awoken on a morning by their sweet sounds as chosen by my mum and dad. I reckon Lennon and McCartney had made a pact with the devil, they'd written so many brilliant songs together, it just wasn't natural. Still, when I was fifteen in 1980, that freak with the pistol made sure Lennon paid for it. There were too many of their tracks to choose from to tell you my favourite - just like with The Stranglers or even with Leeds goals - but if you pushed me, 'Your Mother Should Know' would definitely be in my top ten. It's on their Magical Mystery Tour EP and album. Even though the lyrics are happy, Paul McCartney's voice sounds so sad and from the first line of *'Let's all get up and dance to a song that was a hit before your mother was born, though she was born a long long time ago, Your mother should know ...'* it gave me a shiver down my spine, even more so because it was the song that was playing when I woke up believing I was dead.

Laburnum trees are ugly: spidery branches, wrinkled withered pods and hardly any leaves to speak of. They look like they're always in winter, more dead than alive, even when they're in bloom with coats of yellow blossom and I had the one in our front garden scratching at my bedroom window to add to the effect. What's more, the seeds are poisonous, so me and our kid were always told to steer clear. It's funny that birds don't die when they eat things such as berries that are lethal to us, I always hoped to see piles of dead magpies lying at the foot of the laburnum. I've always hated those little twats, taking over other birds' nests and eating their eggs as well as their chicks even. Nasty pieces of work, magpies. So we never touched the laburnum seeds, we weren't stupid. Never mind not getting a pudding at teatime or being made to miss The Goodies or It's a Knockout, the thought of dying scared us enough. That is, until dicksplash me thought it a good idea to kill myself, just because I fancied Jeni Massey so much it hurt. Even so young, I thought I was in love, except she didn't fancy me one bit. Rejection's hard enough to accept as an adult let alone that age. So-called mates of mine spread my shame around school quicker than shit off a stick, and even if others do quickly forget your embarrassment, permanent scars can occur. It was a humiliating episode for me and I was really upset, pathetic as it might seem. I decided to end my suffering and create some for others by swallowing laburnum seeds: little young green ones and larger, evil looking black ones. And all of this happened before my bollocks had dropped and before my dad had died so talk about over sensitive. I wanted people to feel guilty and to realise what a lovely kid I was and how much they'd miss me. It never entered my head what a selfish uncaring little fucker I was being. Instead of trying to top myself, a good cry or a real heart to heart with my mum might have helped but you're not supposed to show your emotions when you're a lad, you just keep them to yourself.

I couldn't stand the taste, it was worse than the over boiled sick smelling green beans we got in school dinners. The seeds made me shiver when I tasted them and my mouth filled with spit so I just gulped them whole, about fifty in total. I went to bed early that night taking our grimy turquoise bucket from under the kitchen sink with me. I didn't feel any different for ages, 'til I got a warm sensation in my stomach which grew and grew. I started getting dizzy and feeling sick, proper pukesville stuff, and I spent the rest of the night and in to the early hours, puking and puking, and puking. And puking. There was sick coming up with stuff in it I was sure I'd never eaten and I was retching that much I thought I would gip my innards up or turn my guts inside out. When I eventually went to sleep, empty and hollow, I dreamt of me playing for Leeds alongside Peter Lorimer, Norman Hunter and the other heroes, and Tony Currie hitting sixty yard pearlers to me; and there was the Kop singing 'Steve' over and over to me. So come the next morning and I'm still unconscious but somehow hearing my mum playing 'Your Mother Should Know' on the hi-fi, up pop the 'moptop' Beatles presenting the gleaming silver FA Cup to the Leeds team and me and our running around the Wembley pitch parading it. I opened my eyes and blinked in disbelief.

This continued for minutes, lying on my back, me trying to work out where I was. Were the orange wallpaper and the multicoloured lampshade and the Leeds posters on the walls real or was it my Bedroom in Heaven? I was scared to move; I didn't want to be dead. If I'd chewed the seeds rather than swallowed them whole maybe things would've turned out different I don't know, but I had a feeling I'd been rescued or possibly even reprieved.

When I do die, I want it to be a blooming huge funeral. I'd like as many to attend as poss to demonstrate what a popular and much loved bloke I was. Course, I want people to be sad, distraught even, when they hear my clogs have been popped, but after the shock of the news I want them to party and to hold the most colourful and cheerful funeral anyone's ever experienced. It should be seen as a celebration of my next journey to a better place, a higher plain, and I hope one day to meet you there, my friends. I'm not religious (I don't know *what* to believe) but I do feel there's an afterlife or spiritual paradise awaiting our souls. I'll be buried at St Mary's Church opposite the Co-op but the fun will start down the hill on Elland Road in the football stadium, if it's still there. If not, in The Peacock will do. No one will be allowed to wear black (except The Stranglers if, by strange chance, they're still kicking), everyone must wear one colour each - even red despite the Lancashire connections - though brown would be frowned upon and there's too much green already on the scene. The horse drawn hearse will be decked in beautiful and bright flowers, though not tackily with my name in big letters like they are for gangsters or whatever. The music playing all the while will be The Stranglers' 'Walk On By' (the extended version) and 'Love Will Tear Us Apart' by Joy Division. Pete Wylie's 'Sinful' (twelve inch) should make an appearance, too. I hope the residents of Wesley Street will close their curtains as a mark of respect like you're supposed to do, especially with me being a Beeston boy. As well as 'All Things Bright and Beautiful' being sung in St Mary's - it is a church after all - a medley of Stranglers, New Order, Beatles and the Doors' 'Riders on the Storm' should be played please, rounded off by Louis Armstrong's 'What a Wonderful World'. After the service, for the men the day will then begin in earnest. The ladies should not be offended by this, it's just that alcohol will be drunk in copious amounts and even at whatever grand age many of the fellas will be, you know how drink can make them frisky and an erect walking stick has no conscience, don't forget.

We've done a few Half Pint Marathons in our time - supping half a pint in as many pubs as we could - and I'd like this to be The One, the finale. The pubs will probably have different names by then, or even been knocked down *in the name of progress*, but I'd like the following hostelries to be visited, even if we (you) are scratched from them: The Whistlestop, The Old White Hart, along Old Lane to Tommy Wass's, down Dewsbury Road to The Broadway (tap room) and on to The Blooming Rose in Hunslet. The Junction is optional and you can miss The Moorhouse for me, if you like. Taxis will then be necessary - Beeston Line or Gee Gees, keep the local economy alive - for the trip in to town, starting at The Adelphi providing it's Tetley's and a short walk up to the alley where stands The Whip. And after the drinks have been downed in there, trashing the place is a mighty fine idea seeing as it was once a favourite hovel for the NF types. You can forget your 'Mucky Duck' and The Scotsman and The Regent, I was never that attached. Up Briggate there's Whitelocks, The Ship and just around the corner near the Odeon is The Horse and Trumpet. Lower down the Headrow are The Vine and The Three Legs and up on Vicar Lane is The Templar. You might see my old 'mate' Ziggy in there - he'll be the one starting a fight in the mirror or picking on a 'Sal-y' Army lady - and if you do, buy him a pint, gob in it and give it him with my compliments. Make sure he drinks it all, finishing with a hearty lick of the lips. You can kick fuck out of him too then, if you like. At the top of Briggate is The Wrens and if I've shuffled off this mortal coil near to Christmas, make sure you nick the decorations, just for old times' sake. The only other two obligatory visits are The Victoria and The Town Hall Tavern. I say 'only' but these are my two most cherished Leeds haunts even without the existence of jukeboxes and much annie. Around the corner from The Tavern (the 'T H T') is Millgarth Police Station and not only would I deem it a great honour if any of the lads have to spend the night there, I would very possibly live laughing.

Back to this monument down Dewsbury Road: there was nothing for it but for me to have a look at it for myself. I walked down there one summer evening. Past the chippy on Barkly Road and the great modern mansion-like 'Labour' house at the foot of the hill, past Larry's chippy on Barkly Parade and the stretch of Cross Flatts Park and the ancient barbershop (where the cantankerous shit once barked 'No styling' at me when I asked for a side-parting) and the fire station and the Crescent Bingo Hall on the other side of the road, which me and Mike had often tipped as a potential and undiscovered Aladdin's Cave of totty. Soon I was past the enormous old houses on the left with their countless cellars and endless tunnels (so I was told) and finally near the bottom of Dewsbury Road opposite the Junction Hotel. A few yards before the monument, six or seven people were waiting in the pale turquoise bus shelter. I walked on by, deciding not to ask one of them what the monument was about. I was glad I didn't, because it wasn't a monument, it was a bloody clapped out, cushion and padding-less grey armchair with shiny black upholstery. I needed my eyes testing, and my head, just like whoever had gone to all that trouble of carrying and dumping the armchair there. All that trouble ...

Next time if I want to end it all, I'll do it right, with a car exhaust and some rubber tubing (plus car, obviously). Some shocking shit would have to happen though - and I mean seriously shocking - for me to even consider it. Having said that, being the contrary pillock that I am, I do sometimes think about it, if only when I'm dog tired or boozed up and feeling sorry for myself; which goes to show what overdoing something can do for you. As yet, it's not been too strong a temptation, I'm pleased to say. And one positive came out as a result of my attempted suicide: when I wake up on a morning, there's a different song playing in my head every time. I'm not nauseatingly jolly with it as well mind, it's not like I leap out of bed with an idiotic smile on my face, but I tell you, it is a better way to start your day.

My epitaph should be one of the following:-

TOLD YOU I WAS ILL

OR
A GOOD FRIEND WHO NEVER KNOWINGLY
SHAFTED ANYONE
OR SHAT ON HIS MATES

OR
HERE LIES STEVE BOTTOMLEY,
WHO DIED LOADED
or
FAMOUS
or
LAUGHING
or
COMING
or

ALL OF THE ABOVE.

Thanks

This writing malarkey is a bit of a lonely business – solitary confinement might be a better description - but I can't be held *solely* responsible for what's come out of my printer these last few years.

I'd like to thank the people at The Opening Line for inviting me along in those early days and for their subsequent support and guidance; gratitude too to the then lady in my life for initially persuading me to join The Opening Line and for her great encouragement.

Without Ian Duhig in the beginning, Danny Broderick later and editor Steve Dearden at the end, I really do doubt whether 'One Northern Soul' would have got anywhere. Thank you, gents (and not a bloody Leeds fan among 'em - scandalous).

There are way too many people to list individually who have helped, shown genuine interest or simply inspired me but I just have to thank those who have always given me a kick up my Southern region in times of laxness: obviously my Mum, Dad and Graham, and friends ('The Lads' – come on you Flatts!) and workmates who always backed me without ever doubting or discouraging me, including those at BT Cellnet and BT who worked hard and selflessly at their jobs as well as their friendships. And I'm grateful to Ian, Nicole and Dean at Route, for their long running help and kind words.

Something came to light after I'd written 'Terracism', about certain events occurring which the story states *didn't* happen. I'd like to clarify that the stories are from a boy's personal accounts and, in the end, they are works of fiction, not journalism (fiction versus journalism being a completely different kettle of worms, obviously!)

No Cockneys or other animals were hurt in the making of this book.

Robert
www.jrendeacott.btinternet.co.uk

Kilo

M Y Alam

ISBN 1-901927 09 1

Khalil Khan was a good boy. He had a certain past and an equally certain future awaited until gangsters decided to turn his world upside down. They shattered his safe family life with baseball bats but that's just the beginning. They turned good, innocent and honest Khalil into someone else: Kilo, a much more unforgiving and determined piece of work. Kilo cuts his way through the underworld of Bradford street crime, but the closer he gets to the top of that game, the stronger the pull of his original values become. When he finally begins to rub shoulders with the men who inadvertently showed him the allure of crime, the more convinced he becomes that it is sometimes necessary to bad in order to achieve good.

'M Y Alam consistently articulates the experience of dual cultural identity, of being British born with Pakistani heritage and he violently runs this through the mixer with life on the mean streets seasoned with references to hip-hop and American gangster movies.'

The Blackstuff

Val Cale

ISBN 1-901927 14 8

'The mind is like a creamy pint of Guinness…The head is the engine that drives you through the day…the fuel however lies in the blackstuff, in the darkness, in the depths of the unexplored cave which is your subconscious mind…this is the story of my journey through the blackstuff.'

The Blackstuff is a true story of a road-trip that sees Val Cale in trouble in Japan, impaled in Nepal, ripped off at a vaginal freak show in Bangkok, nearly saturated by a masturbating Himalayan bear in the most southerly town of India and culminates in a mad tramp across the world looking for the ultimate blowjob and the meaning of life.

The Blackstuff is *not* just a book. It is *not* just the opinion of an individual who feels that he has something important to say. This is a story which every last one of us can relate to, a story about the incessant battle between our internal angels and our demented demons. This is an odyssey to the liquefied centre of the brain, a magic carpet ride surfing on grass and pills, seas of booze, and the enormous strength of the human soul.

The Blackstuff takes you beyond the beach, deeper into the ocean of darkness that is the pint of stout in your head…

Weatherman
Anthony Cropper
ISBN 1-901927 16 4

Ken sits out the back, in the flatlands that surround Old Goole, and watches the weather. That's what he was doing with poor Lucy, that fateful day, sat on the roof of his house, lifting her up to the sky. Lucy's friend, Florrie, she knew what would happen.

All this is picked up by Alfie de Losinge's machine, which he had designed to control the weather. Instead, amongst the tiny atoms of cloud formations, he receives fragmentary images of events that slowly unfold to reveal a tender, and ultimately tragic, love story.

In this beautifully crafted first novel, Anthony Cropper skilfully draws a picture of life inextricably linked to the environment, the elements, and the ever changing weather.

Very Acme
Adrian Wilson
ISBN: 1 901927 12 1 £6.95

New Nomad, nappy expert, small town man and ultimately a hologram – these are the life roles of Adrian Wilson, hero and author of this book, which when he began writing it, was to become the world's first novel about two and a half streets. He figured that all you ever needed to know could be discovered within a square mile of his room, an easy claim to make by a man who's family hadn't moved an inch in nearly seven centuries.

All this changes when a new job sends him all around the world, stories of Slaughter and the Dogs and Acme Terrace give way to Procter and Gamble and the Russian Mafia. He starts feeling nostalgic for the beginning of the book before he gets to the end.

Very Acme is two books within one, it is about small town life in the global age and trying to keep a sense of identity in a world of multi-corporations and information overload.

Like A Dog To Its Vomit
Daithidh MacEochaidh
ISBN: 1 901927 07 5 £6.95

Somewhere between the text, the intertext and the testosterone find Ron Smith, illiterate book lover, philosopher of non-thought and the head honcho's left-arm man. Watch Ron as he oversees the begging franchise on Gunnarsgate, shares a room with a mouse of the Lacota Sioux and makes love to Tracy back from the dead and still eager to get into his dungarees. There's a virgin giving birth under the stairs, putsch at the taxi rank and Kali, Goddess of Death, is calling. Only Arturo can sort it, but Arturo is travelling. In part two find out how to live in a sock and select sweets from a shop that time forgot and meet a no-holds barred state registered girlfriend. In part three, an author promises truth, but the author is dead - isn't she?

In this complex, stylish and downright dirty novel, Daithidh MacEochaidh belts through underclass underachieving, postponed-modern sacrilege and the more pungent bodily orifices.

Crazy Horse
Susan Everett
ISBN 1 901927 06 7 £6.95

Jenny Barker, like many young women, has a few problems. She is trying to get on with her life, but it isn't easy. She was once buried underneath the sand and it had stopped her growing up, plus she had killed the milkman. Her beloved horse has been stolen while the vicious *Savager* is on the loose cutting up animals in fields. She's neither doing well in college nor in love and fears she may die a virgin.

Crazy Horse is a wacky ride.

Adult Entertainment

Chloe Poems

ISBN 1 901927 18 0 £6.95

One of the most prodigiously gifted and accessible poets alive today, Chloe Poems has been described as 'an extraordinary mixture of Shirley Temple and pornography.' This collection of political and social commentary, first presented in Midsummer 2002, contains twenty-three poems of uncompromising honesty and explicit republicanism, and comes complete with a fourteen track CD of Chloe live in performance.

Half a Pint of Tristram Shandy

Jo Pearson, Daithidh MacEochaidh, Peter Knaggs

ISBN 1 901927 15 6 £6.95

A three-in-one peotry collection from the best in young poets. Between the leaves of this book lies the mad boundless energy of the globe cracking-up under our very noses; it is a world which is harnessed in images of jazz, sex, drugs, aliens, abuse; in effective colloquial language and manic syntax; but the themes are always treated with gravity, unsettling candour and humour.

I Am

Michelle Scally-Clarke

ISBN 1 901927 08 3 £10 Including free CD

At thirty years old, Michelle is the same age as the mother who gave her up into care as a baby. In the quest to find her birth parents, her roots and her own identity, this book traces the journey from care, to adoption, to motherhood, to performer. Using the fragments of her own memory, her poetry and extracts from her adoption files, Michelle rebuilds the picture of 'self' that allows her to transcend adversity and move forward to become the woman she was born to be.

You can hear the beat and song of Michelle Scally-Clarke on the CD that accompanies this book and, on the inside pages, read the story that is the source of that song.

Moveable Type

Rommi Smith

ISBN 1 901927 11 3 £10 Including free CD

It is the theme of discovery that is at the heart of *Moveable Type*. Rommi Smith takes the reader on a journey through identity, language and memory, via England and America, with sharp observation, wit and wry comment en route. The insights and revelations invite us not only to look beneath the surface of the places we live in, but also ourselves. *Moveable Type* and its accompanying CD offer the reader the opportunity to listen or read, read and listen. Either way, you are witnessing a sound that is uniquely Rommi Smith.

Route Subscription

Route's subscription scheme is the easiest way for readers to keep in touch with new work from the best of new writers. Subscribers receive a minimum of four books per year, which could take the form of a novel, an anthology of short stories, a novella, a poetry collection or mix and match titles. Any additional publications and future issues of the route paper will also be mailed direct to subscribers, as well as information on route events and digital projects.

Route constantly strives to promote the best in under represented voices, outside of the mainstream, and will give support to develop promising new talent. By subscribing to route, you too will be supporting these artists.

The fee is modest. UK **£15** Europe **£20 (35€ approx)**
Rest of World **£25(US$40 approx)**

Subscribe online now at www.route-online.com

To receive a postal subscription form email your details to books@route-online.com or send your details to:
route, school lane, glasshoughton, wf10 4qh, uk